"You said...*our* situation," Zoe reminded Raj, keen to steer the conversation out of deep waters. "What did you mean by that?"

"My father has offered me a most unexpected suggestion," Raj said with care, brilliant dark eyes locked to her heart-shaped face and the eyes as bright as emeralds against her porcelain-pale skin. The contrast was breathtaking. "He has asked me to come home and take my place as his heir again."

"My goodness, that's wonderful news! I mean..." Zoe hesitated. "If *that* is what you want..."

"I want to come home with my whole heart. This is the first time I have been home in eight years," Raj admitted harshly, his sincerity bitingly obvious. "But unfortunately, the king's proposition came with a key stipulation attached. My father has asked me to take Hakem's place as your bridegroom and marry you."

Zoe blinked several times and continued to stare at him, her heart thumping rapidly enough that it seemed to thunder in her ears. "But...but why? That's a crazy suggestion!"

Billionaires at the Altar

The world's wealthiest men...redeemed by their innocent brides!

Stamboulas Fotakis will stop at *nothing* to protect his three granddaughters. So, with their reputations in jeopardy, he decides to play matchmaker. Soon, the Mardas sisters find three unexpected billionaires at their doorstep—and they've each brought a diamond ring!

But convincing Winnie, Vivi and Zoe to be their convenient brides isn't going to be easy... If they're to walk down the aisle, then these billionaires must prove that their marriages are more than just business deals. Can the burning intensity of their wedding nights begin to melt the hearts of the world's wealthiest men?

Find out what happens in:

Winnie and Eros's story

The Greek Claims His Shock Heir

Vivi and Raffaele's story

The Italian Demands His Heirs

Zoe and Raj's story

The Sheikh Crowns His Virgin

Available now!

Lynne Graham

THE SHEIKH CROWNS HIS VIRGIN

ISBN-13: 978-1-335-47833-7

The Sheikh Crowns His Virgin

First North American publication 2019

This edition published by arrangement with Harlequin Books S.A.

For questions and comments about the quality of this book, please contact us at CustomerService@Harlequin.com.

Printed in U.S.A.

Lynne Graham was born in Northern Ireland and has been a keen romance reader since her teens. She is very happily married to an understanding husband who has learned to cook since she started to write! Her five children keep her on her toes. She has a very large dog who knocks everything over, a very small terrier who barks a lot and two cats. When time allows, Lynne is a keen gardener.

Books by Lynne Graham

Harlequin Presents

The Italian's Inherited Mistress

Wedlocked!

His Queen by Desert Decree

Billionaires at the Altar

The Greek Claims His Shock Heir
The Italian Demands His Heirs
The Sheikh Crowns His Virgin

Vows for Billionaires

The Secret Valtinos Baby
Castiglione's Pregnant Princess
Da Rocha's Convenient Heir

Visit the Author Profile page at Harlequin.com for more titles.

CHAPTER ONE

ZOE DESCENDED THE steps of her grandfather's private jet and as the sunlight of Maraban enveloped her she smiled happily. It was spring and the heat was bearable but, best of all, she was taking the very first brave step into her new life.

On her own, on her own *at last*, free of the restrictions that her sisters would have attached to her but, most importantly of all, free of the *low* expectations they had of her. Winnie and Vivi had been amazed when Zoe had agreed to move to a foreign country for a few months without freaking out at the prospect. They had been equally amazed when she'd agreed to marry a much older man to fulfil her part of their agreement with their grandfather, Stamboulas Fotakis. Why not? It wasn't as though it was going to be a *real* marriage, merely a pretend marriage in which her future husband made political use of the fact that she was the granddaughter of a former princess of a country called Bania, which no longer existed.

Long before Zoe was even born the two tiny realms of Bania and Mara had joined to become Maraban and apparently her late grandmother, the Princess Azra, had been hugely popular in both countries. Prince Hakem wanted to marry Zoe literally for her ancestry and she would become an Arabian princess and live in the royal palace for several months. There she would enjoy glorious solitude with nobody bothering her, nobody asking how she felt or worriedly enquiring if she thought she should have more therapy to help her cope with ordinary life. Even though she hadn't had a panic attack in months, her siblings had always been on edge around her, awaiting another one.

Zoe adored her older sisters but their constant care and concern had held her back from the independence she needed to rebuild her self-esteem and forge her own path. And taking part in this silly pretend marriage was all she had to do to finally obtain that freedom.

All three sisters had agreed to marry men of their grandfather's choosing to gain his financial help for their foster parents, John and Liz Brooke. Winnie and Vivi had already fulfilled that bargain. But in Zoe's case, no pressure whatsoever had been placed on her and, indeed, John and Liz's mortgage arrears had been paid off shortly after her sister Vivi's marriage had taken place. Yes, she thought wryly, even her extremely ruthless grandfather had shrunk from taking the risk of putting pressure on his youngest granddaughter, having taken on board her siblings' conviction that she was hopelessly fragile and emotionally vulnerable. Nobody had faith in her ability to be strong, Zoe reflected ruefully, which was why it was so very important that she proved for her own benefit that she *could* be strong.

Like her sisters, Zoe had grown up in foster care, and a terrifying incident when she was twelve years old had traumatised her. But she had buried all that hurt and fear, seemingly flourishing in John and Liz's happy home, only for those frightening insecurities to come back and engulf her while she was studying botany at university. Having to freely mix with men, having to deal with friends asking why she didn't want a boyfriend, had put her under severe strain. Her panic attacks had grown worse and worse and, although she had contrived to hide her extreme anxiety from her sisters, she had, ultimately, been unable to deal with her problems alone. Weeks before she sat her final degree exams, she had suffered a nervous breakdown, which had meant that she had had to take time out from her course to recover.

Although she had subsequently completed her degree and worked through the therapy required to put her back on an even track where crippling anxiety no longer ruled her every thought and action, her sisters had continued to treat her as if she could shatter again at any moment. While she understood that their protectiveness came from love, she also saw that their attitude had made her weaker than she need have been and that she badly needed the chance to stand on her own feet. With her sisters now married, one living in Greece and the other in Italy, coming to Maraban was Zoe's opportunity to prove that she had overcome her unhappy past.

Zoe stepped into the limousine awaiting her, grateful for the reality that her arrival in Maraban was completely low-key. Prince Hakem had insisted that no public appearances or indeed anything of that nature would be required from her. He might be the brother of the current King but he had no official standing in Maraban. Zoe's grandfather should have been travelling with her but a pressing business matter had led to him asking if she could manage alone if he put off his arrival until the following day. Of course, she could manage, she thought cheerfully, gazing out with lively interest at the busy streets of the capital city, Tasit, which was an intriguing mix of old and new. She saw old buildings and elaborate mosques with quaint colourful turrets nudging shoulders with redeveloped areas boasting soaring skyscrapers and office blocks. Maraban was evidently right in the middle of the process of modernisation.

Oil and gas wealth had transformed the country. Zoe had read everything she could find on Maraban and had rolled her eyes at the discovery that nobody appeared to know why her grandmother, Princess Azra, had failed to marry the current King, Tahir, as she had been expected to do. The bald truth was that Azra had run off with Stamboulas Fotakis sooner than marry a man who'd already had three wives. Presumably that story had been suppressed to conserve the monarch's dignity. Luckily, Stam had told her everything she needed to know about his late wife's background.

Darkness was falling fast when the limo driver turned off the road and steered between imposingly large gates guarded by soldiers. Zoe strained to see the enormous property that lay ahead but the limo travelled slowly right on past it, threading a path through a vast complex of buildings and finally drawing up beside one. She was ushered out and indoors before she could even catch her breath and was a little disappointed to find herself standing in a contemporary house. A very *large* contemporary house, she conceded wryly, with aggressively gilded fancy furniture and nothing whatsoever historic about it. A female servant in a long kaftan bowed to her and showed her up a brilliantly lit staircase into an entire suite of rooms.

Her disappointment that she wasn't going to be living in the ancient royal palace slowly ebbed as she scanned her comfortable and well-furnished surroundings. It wasn't ideal that none of the staff spoke her language and that she didn't speak theirs but miming could accomplish a lot, she told herself bracingly as her companion mimicked eating to let her know that a meal was being brought. And long before she went home again, she should have picked up at least a few useful phrases to enable her to communicate more effectively, she told herself soothingly.

A maid had already arrived to unpack her suitcases when a knock sounded on the door. Zoe made it to the door first.

A slimly built young man and a uniformed nurse hovered outside. 'I am Dr Wazd,' the man told her stiffly. 'I have been instructed to give you a vaccination shot. The nurse will assist.'

Zoe winced because she hated needles and she was surprised because she had had all the required shots for Maraban. But then what she did know that a medical doctor would not know better? She rolled up her sleeve and then frowned as she saw the doctor's hand on the syringe was shaking. Glancing up at him in surprise, noting the perspiration beading his brow, she wondered if he was a very newly qualified doctor to be so nervous and she was relieved when the nurse silently filched the syringe from him and gave her the injection without further ado. It stung and she gritted her teeth.

No sooner was that done than a tray of food arrived and she sat down at the table to eat, noting that she was feeling dizzy and woolly-headed and surmising that she was already suffering the effects of jet lag. But while she was eating, she began feeling as though the world around her were slowing down and her body felt as heavy as lead. Feeling dizzy even seated, she rose to go to the bathroom and had to grip the back of a chair to balance. As she wobbled on her heels, blinking rapidly, a suffocating blackness folded in and she dropped down into it with a gasp of dismay…

His Royal Highness, Prince Faraj al-Basara, was in a very high-powered meeting in London dealing with his country's oil and gas production when his private mobile thrummed a warning in his pocket. Few people had that number and it only ever rang if it was very, *very* important. Excusing himself immediately, Raj stepped outside, his brain awash with sudden apprehension. Had his father taken ill? Or had some other calamity occurred back home in Maraban?

Maraban was a tiny Gulf state but it was also one of the richest countries in the world. A terrorist incident, however, would bring the home of his birth to a screeching halt because the security forces were equally tiny and these days Maraban relied on wealth and diplomacy to stay safe. When

Raj thought nostalgically of home, it was always of a place of stark black and white contrasts where four-wheel-drive vehicles and helicopters startled livestock in the desert and where a conservative Middle Eastern ethos struggled to cope with the very different mores and the sheer speed of change in the modern world.

It was eight years, however, since Raj had last visited his home because his father, the King, had removed him from his position as Crown Prince and sent him into exile for refusing to go into the army and for refusing even more vehemently to marry the bride his parent had chosen for him. No, he had not been a dutiful or obedient son, Raj acknowledged with grim self-honesty, he had been a stubborn, rebellious one and, unfortunately for him, there was no greater sin in his culture.

That said, however, Raj had, since, moved on from that less than stellar beginning to carve his own path in the business world and there his shrewd brain, intuition and ability to spot trends had ensured meteoric success in that sphere. He had also learned how to steer Maraban into the future from beyond its borders, making allies, attracting foreign businesses and investment while constantly encouraging growth in the public infrastructure required to keep his country up to speed with the latest technology. And his reward for that tireless focus and resolve? Maraban, the home that he loved, was positively booming.

He was pleasantly surprised when he answered his phone and recognised his cousin, Omar's voice. Omar had pretty much been his best friend since the dark days of the military school they had both been forced to attend as adolescents, an unforgettable era of relentless bullying and abuse that Raj still winced to recall. As Crown Prince he had had a target painted on his back and his father had told the staff to turn a blind eye, believing that it would be beneficial for his only child to be toughened up in such a severe environment.

'Omar…what can I do for you?' he asked almost cheerfully, relieved of the anxiety that his elderly father had taken ill because Omar would not have been chosen as messenger for that development. *That* call would only have come from a member of his father's staff. After all, his mother had died while he was still a boy. The memory made him tense for his mother had died in a manner that he would never forget: she had taken her own life. It had taken a very long time for Raj to accept that her unhappiness had surpassed her love for her nine-year-old son and he had never forgotten his sense of abandonment because, once she was gone, everything soft and loving and caring had vanished from his childish world.

'I'm in a real fix, Raj, and I think you are the

only person with sufficient knowledge to approach with this,' Omar declared, his habitually upbeat voice unusually flat in tone. 'I've been dragged into something I don't want to be involved in and it's serious. You know I'm a royalist and very loyal to my country but there are some things I *can't*—'

'Cut to the chase,' Raj sliced in with a bemused frown. 'What have you been dragged into?'

'Early this morning I received a call from someone at the palace who asked if I would look after a "package" and keep it safe until further notice. And that's the problem, Raj… I didn't get delivered a package, I got a woman.'

'A *woman*?' Raj repeated in disbelief. 'Are you joking me?'

'I wish I was. All the women in the tribe are outraged and I've been thrown out of my tent to accommodate her,' Omar lamented. 'My wife thinks I'm getting involved in sex trafficking.'

'It could *not* be that,' Raj pronounced with assurance because the penalty for such a crime was death and his father was most assiduous in ensuring that neither drugs nor prostitution gained ground in Maraban.

'No, of course it couldn't be,' Omar agreed. 'But even though the order came from the very highest level of the palace I should not be asked by *anyone* to imprison a woman against her will.'

'How do you know the order came from the very highest level?' Raj demanded.

His cousin mentioned a name and Raj gritted his teeth. Bahadur Abdi was the most trusted military adviser in his father's inner circle and could only be acting at the King's command. That shocking truth shed an entirely different light on the kidnapping because it meant that Raj's father was personally involved. 'Who the hell *is* this woman?'

'You're not going to like the suspicion I'm developing any more than I do,' his cousin warned him heavily. 'But I contacted the palace as soon as I appreciated I was being asked to deal with a *live* package and I was told that she was the last descendant of the al-Mishaal family, which was a shock. Thought they were all dead and buried long ago! Were you even aware that *my* father divorced my mother two months ago?'

Raj was shocked enough by both those revelations to listen keenly as Omar described his mother's refusal to discuss the divorce and the oddity of her continuing calm over the termination of a marriage that had lasted almost fifty years and had spawned four children and at least a dozen grandchildren. Prince Hakem, Raj's uncle and Omar's father, however, was an embittered and ambitious man, who ever since Raj's exile had been striving to become the recognised heir to the throne in Raj's place. Ironically, Raj didn't even really feel that he could blame his uncle for his ambition because, as the King's younger brother, Hakem had spent his whole life close to the throne but virtually ignored and powerless, his royal brother refusing to grant him any form of responsibility in the kingdom. Furthermore, only the King could name his heir and Hakem had long desired a role of power and the rise in status it would accord him.

'So, what's the connection with this woman?'

Omar shared his suspicions and Raj paled and experienced a spontaneous surge of rage at such a manipulative plot being played out in virtual secret behind the palace walls. 'Surely that is *not* possible?'

'It may not be. I must admit that the woman doesn't look remotely as if she carries Marabanian blood. She's got white-blonde hair...looks like something out of that fairy tale... *The Sleeping Beauty*,' Omar revealed heavily.

Raj parted compressed lips. 'Princess Azra of Bania was the daughter of a Danish explorer, who was blond,' he murmured flatly. 'I don't know much about Azra's elopement with her Greek tycoon, who was working in Maraban when the two countries joined, but I do know her flight with another man created a *huge* scandal. She was supposed to become my father's fourth wife and instead, she ran off with Fotakis and married him.'

'Didn't know that...but then it's not really my

slice of history in the same way as it's yours.' Omar sighed heavily. 'Just give me some diplomatic advice about what to do next because I'm at a standstill. This woman has *obviously* been kidnapped. Our doctor says she's been drugged, so she's unconscious and she arrived with no means of identification. But even if she *is* one of the al-Mishaal family's next generation from that marriage all those years ago I still can't believe that any *young* woman would agree to marry a man as old as my father—'

'It would shock you what some Western women would be willing to do to become an Arabian princess with unlimited wealth at their disposal. Suggest that a crown could also be on offer and there would be many takers of that particular bargain,' Raj breathed with cynical derision, his lean, darkly handsome features clenching hard as he reflected on his own experiences and the shattering betrayal he had endured...and worst of all, only *after* he had destroyed his standing with his father for ever. Even years after that youthful disillusionment, he was grimly aware of the pulling power of his status and wealth in the West. In his radius even seemingly intelligent women frothed and gushed like champagne, desperate to attract and bed him. Sadly for them, he didn't find being chased, flattered or potentially seduced remotely attractive because he preferred to do his own hunting in that field. And, almost inevitably, that shattering act of infidelity following on from his mother's suicide had underlined his growing conviction that women were not to be trusted.

'Possibly not...shocked,' Omar clarified as tactfully as he knew how because he too was probably thinking about that old and demeaning history that still scarred Raj's pride. 'But I *can* tell you that if that is my father's game, very few of our people would like or accept such a marriage. My father is unpopular: he's as old school as your father. I don't know anyone who would be willing to accept him as the heir in place of you, *no*, not even if he *has* somehow contrived to bring back the ghost of the al-Mishaal royal family as a potential bride!'

Raj had been away from palace politics for a very long time but he had not forgotten the scheming games of one-upmanship involved. In the role of Hakem's bride, Princess Azra's granddaughter would be a priceless figurehead, Raj acknowledged grimly. Half the population of Maraban came from Banian roots and all had been seriously dissatisfied forty-odd years ago when the joining of the two states was not matched as had been promised by a marital alliance between Bania's only Princess and Mara's King. All those people had felt cheated by the absence of Banian blood in the royal family tree of Maraban. It would be a triumph for his uncle to marry Azra's descendant and it definitely would increase his popularity, which was precisely why Raj's father would never have allowed such a marriage to take place: King Tahir did not tolerate competition or, for that matter, a little brother he deemed to be getting too big for his boots. After such a publicity-grabbing stunt, Hakem could only have been hoping to be named the King's heir and step into Raj's former position as Crown Prince in his nephew's stead.

Omar broke into Raj's racing thoughts. 'Tell me, what am I to do with her?' he demanded, infuriated that an innocent woman had been kidnapped to prevent a marriage he believed to be wholly inappropriate. 'How do I safely *and* decently rid myself of this appalling responsibility? '

And Raj told him with a succinctness that shook both of them before he powered back into his meeting to apologise and explain that a family crisis demanded his immediate attention. He contacted an investigation firm, who had done excellent work for him in the past, to request an immediate file on his uncle's putative bride. He needed information and he needed it fast yet he was aware that he was struggling to concentrate.

Why?

For the first time in eight years, Raj would be returning to the country of his birth and, although anger was driving him at the prospect of being forced to deal with another unscrupulous and mercenary woman, on another much more basic level he was quietly exhilarated at the prospect of seeing his homeland again…

Zoe surfaced from an uneasy, woozy dream to find someone helping her to lift a glass of water to her lips. Her eyes refused to focus and her body felt limp but she knew she needed the bathroom and said so. Someone helped her rise and supported her—more than one someone, she registered dimly, because her limbs were too weak to carry her. She tried to scan her surroundings but the walls being weirdly bendy spooked her and momentarily she shut her eyes as she was helped back to bed. She had been drugged, taken somewhere, she registered fearfully, fighting without success to stay conscious and focus. She had to protect herself, *had* to protect herself! That self-saving litany rang through her brain like a wake-up call…but even that panic couldn't prevent her from sliding down into oblivion again.

When Raj received the info on Zoe Mardas, he was forced to rapidly rearrange his expectations. Why on earth would such a woman be willing to marry a man almost as old as her grandfather? Clearly, financial greed would be a most unlikely motive for a woman with the billionaire Stamboulas Fotakis at her back. Fotakis was her grandfather and, by all accounts, an extremely protective relative. Other more stressful concerns then started dawning on Raj. The Greek tycoon would scarcely take the kidnapping of his granddaughter lying down. He would not allow it to be hushed up either. Yet, even more strangely, it did look as though Fotakis had been the prime mover and shaker behind the proposed marriage between Hakem and Zoe. What was Stam Fotakis getting out of it? Some lucrative business deal? Or a title for his granddaughter? Raj pondered those unknowns and decided to contact Fotakis direct…

Someone was brushing Zoe's hair when she next woke up, someone murmuring softly in a foreign language. She opened her eyes and saw an older woman, who smiled down at her from her kneeling stance by her side while she brushed Zoe's long mane of pale blonde hair with admiring care. She did not seem hostile or threatening in any way and Zoe forced a smile, her innate survival instincts kicking in. Until she knew what was happening she would be a good little prisoner, playing along until such time as her grandfather came to rescue her; because one thing she *did* know: Stamboulas Fotakis would not be long in putting in an appearance. He would create a huge fuss the instant he realised that Zoe had gone missing and no rock would be left unturned in his search for her, she reflected with a strong sense of relief.

Gently detaching her hair from the woman's light hold, she sat up and the woman stood up and helpfully showed her straight to the bathroom. Even by that stage, Zoe was recognising that she had not been disorientated the night before when she had thought the walls surrounding her looked rather odd. Evidently, she was no longer at the villa in the palace complex, she was in a tent, a very large and very luxurious tent decorated with rich hangings and opulent seating but, when all was said and done, it was *still* a tent! And the connecting bathroom was also under canvas. Zoe felt hot and sweaty and looked longingly at the shower, but she didn't want to risk the vulnerability of getting naked. She freshened up with cold water, dried her face and frowned down at the unfamiliar long white fine cotton shift she now wore in place of the skirt and top she had travelled in. That creepy nervous doctor and his sidekick, she thought in disgust. She would never trust a doctor again!

Why had she been taken from Prince Hakem's villa? Although no one had ever told her that it was *his* villa, she had simply assumed it was. Presumably somebody didn't want this marriage of his to take place, she reasoned reflectively. No problem, she thought ruefully, there had been no need to assault her with a syringe, send her to sleep and ship her out to a tent because she would quite happily go home again without any argument. Furthermore, she rather thought that would be her grandfather's reaction as well because he had demanded very strong assurances from her bridegroom-to-be that she would be safe and secure in Maraban and he would be appalled at what had happened to her. Surely her becoming a princess to follow in the footsteps of her formerly royal grandmother, Princess Azra, would not still be so important to Stam Fotakis that he would expect his granddaughter to risk life and limb in the process?

Two women were setting out a meal when she returned to the main tent and she roamed as casually as she could in the direction of the doorway that had been left uncovered. What she glimpsed froze her in her tracks in instant denial. She saw a circle of tents and beyond them sand dunes that ran off into the horizon. She was in the desert, so escaping would be more of a challenge than she felt equal to because she would need transport and a map at the very least for such a venture. The discovery that she had been plunged into such an alien environment sent her nervous tension climbing higher and she swallowed hard. Where else had she expected a tent to be pitched but in the desert? she asked herself irritably.

Above one of the tents she espied the rotor blades of a helicopter. Was that how she had arrived? Had she been flown in? She shuddered as another far more frightening thought suddenly occurred to her.

Why was she assuming that she had been kidnapped to prevent the wedding taking place in forty-eight hours? Her grandfather was an extremely rich man. It was equally possible that she had been taken so that a ransom demand could be made for her release. That scenario meant that someone laying violent hands on her was a much more likely development, she decided sickly, her tummy hollowing out. As one of the women carefully threaded her stiff arms into a concealing wrap and even tied it for her, Zoe could feel all the hallmarks of an impending panic attack assailing her and she was already zoning out as her thoughts raged out of her control.

She saw a mental image of herself beaten up in a photo for her grandfather's benefit. Her heart raced and she turned rapidly away from the view of the encampment, incapable of even noticing that the two women with her were hastily bowing and backing out of the tent again or that a male figure now stood silhouetted in the doorway. Her throat was tight, making it hard for her to catch her breath. She was shivering in spite of the heat, cold, then hot, dizziness making her sway as panic threatened.

I'm fine, I'm strong, I can cope, she chanted

inwardly. But the mantra that usually worked to steady her failed because for several unbearable seconds she was simply overpowered by fear.

A male voice sounded directly behind her and a hand brushed her shoulder. Startled, terrified, Zoe reacted automatically with the self-defence tactics she had spent months learning so that she had the skills she needed to ensure her personal safety.

She spun at speed, her elbow travelling up for a chest blow and her clenched fist heading for a throat strike while her knee lifted to aim at the groin. Raj was so disconcerted by a woman the size of a child attacking him that he almost fell over in sheer shock and then his own training kicked in and, light as dancer on his feet, he twisted and blocked her before bringing her down on the rug beneath their feet with careful hands.

'Let go of me, you bastard!' she railed at him, clawing, biting and scratching and in the act contriving to dislodge the white *keffiyeh* that covered his head.

Still reeling with disconcertion, Raj backed off several steps because he couldn't subdue her without hurting her and he refused to take that risk. She squirmed frantically away and the sheer terror in her face savaged his view of himself. Her eyes were glassy, her face white as snow.

'You are quite safe here. Nobody is going to hurt you.' Raj crouched down to her level while she wriggled back against a carved wooden chest like a trapped animal and hugged her knees, rocking back and forth. She was tiny and his every instinct was to protect her. 'On my honour, I *swear* that you are safe…' he intoned with as much conviction as he could get into the assurance, because she wasn't listening to him and she wasn't looking at him.

He was annoyed that his cousin had not sent his English-speaking wife, Farida, in to Zoe immediately to explain that there was no threat of any kind against her. But most of all, he cursed his father and the omnipotence he wielded in Maraban, for Raj was convinced that his wily father had ordered the kidnapping of Hakem's youthful bride-to-be. Would his father have counted the cost to the woman involved? Would he even have foreseen that he was unleashing the kind of explosively damaging scandal that no self-respecting country could withstand? No, his father, Tahir, would not have looked at that bigger picture of cause and effect. He would simply have set out to ensure that his ambitious brother's plot to raise his status was foiled while steadfastly refusing to acknowledge the likelihood of unexpected consequences.

In a fierce temper at that frustrating knowledge, Raj sank down beside Zoe Mardas on his knees and began to coax her into attempting a breathing exercise, aimed at calming her down. Extraordinary green eyes, clear as emeralds, skimmed over him and she blinked, long feathery lashes dipping. For a split second he was frozen in place by her ice-cool Scandinavian beauty. He coached her in breathing in, holding her breath and then very slowly breathing out again. She did so and then shot him an exasperated look, *not* the kind of look Raj was accustomed to receiving from young women.

'Yes, I do know how to do that for myself!' Zoe told him sharply as soon as she was breathing normally again. 'Why do you know how?'

'For a while in my teens, I suffered similar episodes,' Raj admitted, startling himself with that candour as much as he startled her; for the severe bullying he had endured at military school had for years afterwards left him damaged. He could only think his candour had been unwisely drawn from him by his glimpse of her at her most vulnerable and a natural need to put her at her ease.

In receipt of that surprising admission, Zoe stared back at him in wonderment because in her experience men were much less willing to admit to suffering such a condition. But before she could question him further to satisfy her curiosity, he vaulted gracefully upright again. She watched him smooth down his rumpled white buttoned tunic and snatch up the white head cloth she had dislodged in their tussle. And then, strikingly, for the first time in her life Zoe looked at a man with interest because there was no denying it: whoever he was, he was without question the most beautiful creature she had ever seen. Dense silky blue-black curls covered his well-shaped skull while high cheekbones and hollows fed into a truly spectacular bone structure sheathed in olive skin. Dark-as-the-devil eyes glittered below straight ebony brows. A faint shadow of stubble surrounded his wide sensual mouth, his full soft lower lip tensing as he noticed her lingering scrutiny.

Turning pink, Zoe hurriedly glanced away while scolding herself for staring but, really, with looks of that quality, he had to be accustomed to being stared at by women, she reasoned defensively, uneasy with her speeded-up heartbeat and the sudden tightening of her nipples.

She wasn't *that* sort of woman, she reminded herself resolutely. Sex didn't interest her. Basically, men didn't interest her. She had been thrown off the path of normal development at the age of twelve when an attempted rape had devastated her. Ever since then she had held herself apart, avoiding mixed company unless it was family-orientated. She was perfectly happy around her brothers-in-law, Eros and Raffaele, and she hadn't been nervous either when dealing with the male parents at the childcare nursery where she had worked for months immediately after her recovery from her breakdown. Back then a full-time job in her own field of botany had seemed too challenging as a first step back into the real world.

'Who are you?' she asked baldly.

'You may call me Raj. I am no one of importance here,' he intoned in smooth dismissal, for he intended to fly back out of Maraban within the hour because he could not risk discovery and possible arrest. 'But this nomadic base camp is where my cousin, Sheikh Omar, lives at this time of year.'

Zoe bridled as she scrambled upright, wishing for about the thousandth time that she was even a few inches taller, for being only four feet eleven inches tall was not an advantage when it came to persuading people to take her seriously. Unsurprisingly, Raj towered over her but he wasn't quite as tall as her brothers-in-law, both of whom put her in mind of giants when she was around them. 'Is he the man responsible for bringing me here… *against my will*?' she stressed acidly.

'No, he is not,' Raj told her emphatically. 'Nor would he harm a hair on your head but he has kept his distance because he does not speak English.'

'Then who *is* responsible for bringing me here?' Zoe demanded, standing her ground, tensing her spine to keep her back and shoulders straight and her head high. Her favourite self-help book urged that even if you didn't *feel* confident, it was still possible to fake confidence and by so doing actually acquire it.

'I'm afraid I can't tell you that,' Raj countered flatly.

Zoe's green eyes flared as if he had slapped her. *'Why not?'* she demanded.

'It would serve no useful purpose.'

Zoe breathed in very deeply to contain the temper she hadn't known she had until that moment. He was so incredibly patronising, so superior and his attitude affected her like a chalk scraping down a blackboard, setting her teeth on edge. 'That's my decision to make, *not* yours,' she said succinctly.

Engaged in replacing his *keffiyeh*, Raj looked heavenward, involuntarily amused by that argument. She was like a doll with that tiny stature of hers and her phenomenally long blonde hair and she barely reached his chest.

'You're not taking me seriously,' she condemned.

'I'm afraid not,' Raj conceded grudgingly. 'I arrived here to sort this unfortunate mess out and that is what I intend to do.'

'Is it indeed?' Zoe snapped, incredulous that he had simply admitted his inability to treat her like an intelligent individual because, in her experience, most people lied on that score, denying that her diminutive size coloured their attitude towards her.

Raj paced several steps away from her, having

discovered that proximity was unwise. His attention kept on dropping to that soft full pink mouth, that shimmering fall of pale hair, the barely noticeable little feminine curves hinting at her physical shape beneath the robe. He shifted, a kick of lust at his groin exasperating him for it was inappropriate and Raj was *always* very appropriate in his reactions to women. He controlled his responses, he did not allow them to control him and he had never understood the intoxicating lust that he had heard other men talk about, because only one woman had ever tested his control and, even then, it had not overwhelmed him.

'I intend to have you conveyed home as soon as it is possible...unless you are unwilling to give up the possibility of marrying my uncle, Prince Hakem, and becoming a princess,' Raj murmured bluntly. 'I suspect my aunt, his wife of many years, whom he recently divorced, would be relieved to have the ingrate back by default, little though he deserves her forgiveness and understanding...'

CHAPTER TWO

'ARE YOU TELLING me that Prince Hakem was already married at the time he agreed to marry me?' Zoe gasped in astonished disbelief, her triangular face tightening and losing colour at that horrendous concept.

'Of course, you were *already* aware of that reality,' Raj informed her with considerable scorn in his tone. 'After all, he has been married for many years. He has four children and a very large number of grandchildren… However, I assume that your grandfather was unwilling to accept a polygamous marriage, so my uncle *had* to divorce his wife before he could be allowed to marry you…'

Zoe was stunned by what she was learning. She wondered if her grandfather had been aware of those same unpleasant facts and then she told herself off for shying away from the unlovely truth that Stam Fotakis had wanted his granddaughter to become a princess regardless of what it would take to achieve that end. Prince Hakem had *had* to divorce his wife to take Princess Azra's granddaughter as a bride! Zoe was appalled and mortified and guilt-stricken, feeling that she should've done her homework better and shouldn't be in the position of finding out such a crucial fact when it was too late to change anything. Hakem's poor wife! Raj was definitely correct in his conviction that her grandfather would never have accepted a polygamous marriage and would only ever have settled for his grandchild becoming the Prince's sole wife.

'I didn't know… I *swear* I didn't know that he was a married man!' Zoe protested vehemently, a guilty flush driving off her previous pallor. 'In spite of what you seem to think, I would never have agreed if I had known that he was getting rid of his real wife just to marry me for a few months.'

Raj had no idea why she was bothering to defend her behaviour by pleading ignorance of the reality that his uncle had been a perfectly happy married man before her availability had ignited his ambition. Zoe Mardas might look convincingly like a storybook princess or a heavenly angel, but Raj had an innate distrust of that level of physical beauty and a cynical view of humanity. Beautiful on the outside but what less than presentable motives were she striving to conceal from him? He had discovered for himself that beautiful on the outside too often meant ugly on the inside.

In any case, Zoe could not possibly be as naïve

as she was pretending to be. She *had* to know her own worth in Marabanian terms. Thousands of delighted Banians would flood the streets to celebrate an alliance between a royal Prince and Princess Azra's grandchild. His uncle had come very close to pulling off a spectacular coup in the popularity stakes.

'I assume you are willing to go home now?' Raj queried, marvelling at his own restraint in asking her that question because, frankly, he was determined to get her out of Maraban by any means within his power.

'Of course, I'm willing to go home!' Zoe shot back at him in reproach. 'Good grief, I'm not wanting to marry a man I've never even met, who divorced his wife just to become my bridegroom! Do I look that desperate?'

'I don't know you. I have no idea what your motivations are or, indeed, *were*,' Raj parried with the intrinsic hauteur that came as naturally to him as breathing, his exotically high cheekbones taut, his arrogant nose lifted, his hard jaw clenched.

Zoe's colour heightened, her eyes brightening with anger, for in a couple of sentences, he had cut her down to size, enforcing the distance between them while also underlining his indifference to her feelings about anything. He looked different with that headdress covering his riot of coal-black curls. While the *keffiyeh* framed and accentuated his superb bone structure and those dark deep-set eyes set below slashing ebony brows, it also made him look older and off-puttingly sombre.

'I confess that I am surprised, however, that you have not even met Prince Hakem. While such traditional matches still occasionally occur in Maraban, they are no longer the norm and I would not have thought a woman from your background would have been prepared to accept a husband sight unseen,' he admitted smoothly, dark eyes glittering back at her in cool challenge.

A wild surge of temper rocked Zoe where she stood, thoroughly disconcerting her, and her small hands coiled into tight fists by her side. The derision lacing his intonation and his appraisal was like a slap in the face. He might say that he didn't know her but she could see that, regardless of that reality, he had still made unsavoury assumptions about her character.

'Who the hell do you think you are to talk to me like this?' Zoe suddenly hissed at him, out of all patience and restraint because the way he was looking at her, as though she were some sort of lesser being, infuriated her. 'I came to this wretched country in good faith and my trust has been betrayed. I was drugged, *kidnapped* and subjected to a terrifying experience! Now you start judging me even though you don't know the facts.'

'I agree that I don't know the facts, nor do I

need to know them,' Raj countered, disconcerted by the passion etched in her heart-shaped face as she answered him back. He wasn't used to that—he wasn't used to that kind of treatment at all.

He had been reserved from childhood, discouraged from letting his guard down with anyone, continually reminded about *who* he was and *what* he was and exactly what his rank demanded. After his mother's tragic death, he had had to learn to conceal his feelings and his insecurities, had had to accept that such personal responses were out of step with his status. An accident of birth had imprisoned him in a separate category, denying him the relaxation of true friends or freedom. When he had finally broken out of that prison, he had discovered to his consternation that that often icy reserve of his, which kept people at a distance, was as much a natural part of him as his face.

'Well, you're going to hear the facts, whether you want to or not!' Zoe snapped back at him curtly. 'Prince Hakem approached my grandfather to suggest the marriage, *not* the other way round. I didn't meet him beforehand because there was no need for me to meet him when it was never intended to be a normal marriage. I was to go through the ceremony and live quietly afterwards in the Prince's home. He swore that he would treat me like a daughter and that no demands would be made of me. Then after several months I was to go home and get a divorce…'

Raj's spectacular eyes gleamed as darkly bright as polar stars while he absorbed that surprising information. He understood now why his aunt had agreed to the divorce without making a fuss. Hakem must have promised to remarry her once he was free again and, in support of her husband's royal ambitions, Raj's aunt had been willing to make that sacrifice. 'But what was in this peculiar arrangement for you?' Raj persisted with a frown of bewilderment. 'It cannot surely have been enriching yourself when your grandfather is such a wealthy man…'

'Status!' Zoe almost spat out the word as if it physically hurt her and, indeed, it did. 'I would've become a princess and, while that doesn't matter much to me, it means a great deal to my grandfather and I wanted to please him. He's done a lot for me and my sisters.'

'Being a princess wouldn't have been much of a consolation while you were living in Hakem's home,' Raj informed her very drily. 'Hakem's wife and children are well known and well liked and everyone who knew them would have been ready to loathe you on sight.'

'Well, the marriage is not going to take place now, is it?' Zoe cut in thinly, turning away from him to wander across to the far side of the tent. 'After all that's happened, *nothing* short of handcuffs and chains would persuade me to stay in Maraban!'

Raj was disconcerted to find his brain sketching an erotic mental image of her chained to a bed, all flyaway blonde hair, passionate green eyes and little heaving pale pink curves for his private delectation. He stiffened and shifted restlessly while he fought to kill that untimely vision stone dead. But, sadly for him, there was nothing politically correct about his body and within seconds he was filled with desire.

'You know, I don't want to be rude or melodramatic,' Zoe began shakily.

'You may not want to be but you can't help behaving that way?' Raj incised hoarsely, knocked off balance now by his libido, that intimate imagery of her strengthening rather than fading and exercising the most extraordinary power over him.

Zoe spun. 'You're the one being rude!' she condemned, challenged to catch her breath when she clashed involuntarily with his intense gaze. 'Acting like being kidnapped is normal and refusing to tell me who orchestrated this whole stupid charade!'

'I am withholding that information because there is *no* possibility of the man involved being punished,' Raj admitted hoarsely.

What was it about that jet-dark gaze that made goose bumps rise on her exposed skin and sent little shivers running down her taut spine? Why did she suddenly feel so ridiculously overheated? Why did her tummy feel as though butterflies were fluttering through it? Instinctively she pressed her thighs together on the ache low in her core and she blinked in bewilderment and growing self-consciousness, her colour heightening as the explanation for her reaction dawned on her and shot through her like a lightning bolt. It was attraction, simple sexual attraction, and she was experiencing it for the first time *ever*. It made her feel all jumpy and twitchy, like a cat trying to walk across hot burning coals. Sheer shock crashed through her slender frame as she endeavoured to rise above her inner turmoil and focus on the conversation.

'And why is there no possibility of punishment?' Zoe demanded boldly.

'I will not discuss that with you. Please get dressed and we will leave.'

'To go where?' Zoe demanded in surprise.

'We are flying first to Dubai and then on to London, where you will be reunited with your grandfather,' Raj explained. 'As that arrangement is acceptable to him, I assume it is equally acceptable to you.'

'Acceptable?' Zoe echoed and she moved forward with a frown, her astonishment unhidden. 'Are you telling me that you have actually *spoken* to Grandad?'

'Of course.' Raj's intonation was clipped and

businesslike. 'He was very angry about your disappearance and I had to reassure him that you were safe and that I would personally ensure that you are restored to his protection as soon as possible.'

But Zoe was still struggling to come to terms with the startling reality that he had already discussed the entire episode with her grandfather because that he should have boldly taken that step was utterly unexpected. Most people avoided Stam Fotakis in a temper and tried to wriggle out of accepting responsibility for anything that annoyed the older man. In fact, the only person she knew who ever stood toe to toe with her grandfather when he was in a bad mood was her sister, Vivi, whose temper matched his. Whoever Raj was, he was fearless, she decided enviously, for when her grandfather started roaring like an angry bull, Zoe simply wanted to keep her head down and take cover.

'I'm in a hurry. We will leave as soon as you are ready. My time here is limited,' Raj admitted flatly, tension tightening his smooth bronzed features. 'I would be obliged if you would be quick.'

'Well, I would need my clothes back to be quick, and I don't know where they are,' Zoe told him thinly, lifting her chin.

With an exclamation, he strode to the doorway and, a moment later, a little woman in tribal dress came running to do his bidding. Zoe's garments were located and laid in her arms, freshly laundered and fragrant. She stalked into the bathroom to look longingly at the shower and then she thought defiantly, What the hell? I'm not putting on clean clothes unless I'm clean as well!

As Zoe stepped beneath the flowing water with a deep sigh of relief, Raj strode out of the main tent, the old rules of polite conduct kicking in even though it felt like a lifetime since he had had to pay attention to such outdated beliefs. She was a single woman and he was a single man and he was in a very old-fashioned place where only his rank had granted him the right to speak to her alone. Even so, he had noted that the females in Omar's family were hovering nearby to ensure that the proprieties were observed. He was relieved that her attack on him had gone unnoticed for that would have very much shocked the tribe, none of whom would have recognised the need for a woman to learn the skills to protect herself. Male relatives were supposed to protect the women in the family.

Evidently, however, Zoe Mardas had not been protected, Raj reckoned thoughtfully, wondering what had happened to her, wondering why she had been so terrified and acknowledging that he would never know. He didn't get into deep conversations of that nature with women. His relationships, if they could be called that, were superficial and consisted of lots of sex and not much else. He doubted that he would ever want anything more from a woman. Why would he? Love had once made him stupid. He had given up everything for love and had ended up with nothing but the crushing awareness that he had made a serious mistake.

'Raj!' Omar gasped as he surged up to him, red-faced from the effort and winded, a small, rather tubby man, who rarely hurried at anything he did. 'You need to leave. One of the camel traders phoned to tell me…a bunch of military helicopters are flying in.'

'Soldiers love to rehearse disasters. It'll be some war game or something,' Raj forecast, refusing to panic. 'I told Zoe to hurry as politely as I could but you know what women are…'

'Raj, if you're caught on Marabanian soil, you could be arrested, *imprisoned*!' Omar emphasised in frustration. 'Grab that stupid woman and get in that helicopter and go!'

The racket of rotor blades approaching made both men throw their heads back and peer into the sky.

'Do you see those colours? That is the royal fleet, which means your father is on board!' Omar groaned in horror.

'It's too late to run. I'll have to tough it out.'

'No, *run*!' Omar urged abruptly. 'Right now… leave the woman here. I think this was a trap. I think she was dumped with me because they knew I was sure to ask you for your help. In the name of

Allah, Raj, I will never forgive myself if you come to harm because of my thoughtlessness!'

A trap? Raj pondered the idea and as quickly discarded it. Why would his father, who had considered him a disappointment practically from the day of his birth, seek to trap him in Maraban? Sending Raj into exile, finally freeing himself from a son and heir who enraged him, had been the best solution for both of them, Raj reasoned ruefully.

'My father always warned me that Tahir was very devious, *very* calculating,' Omar breathed worriedly.

'He is,' Raj agreed. 'But he has no reason to *want* to find his son breaking the terms of his exile. Why would he? That would only embarrass him. I'll stay out of sight. Ten to one, he's taken one of his notions to call a tribal meeting and hash over boundaries and camel disputes. He revels in that kind of stuff…it takes him back to his youth.'

'The army craft are encircling the camp to land in advance,' Omar informed him.

'Standard security with the monarch on board,' Raj dismissed.

'No, I'm telling you,' Omar declared in growing frustration at his friend's lack of concern. 'This was a trap and I don't know how you're going to get out of it…'

CHAPTER THREE

THE RACKET OF the helicopters nearby unnerved Zoe and she dressed in haste, flinching from the cling of her clothes to her still-damp skin. When a woman entered the bathroom to fetch her, she was grateful she had hurried and she walked out through the main tent, glad to be embarking on her journey home.

It was a surprise, however, when she was not escorted to the stationary helicopter she had espied earlier and was instead led into another tent, where a group of women were seated round a campfire.

'The King is visiting,' the woman opposite her explained to her in perfect English. 'My husband, Omar, can only receive the King in his tent, which is, unfortunately, the one you have been using, which means that you will have to wait here with us.'

'Your husband?' Zoe studied the attractive brunette, who wore more gold jewellery than she had ever seen on one woman at the same time.

'Sheikh Omar. The King is his uncle. I am called Farida…and you?'

'Zoe,' Zoe proffered, accepting the tiny cup of black coffee and the plate of sliced fruit she was given with a grateful smile. 'Thank you.'

Hopefully she would be on her way home within the hour, she reasoned, munching on a slice of apple with appetite. 'Where's Raj?' she asked curiously. 'I thought he was in a hurry to leave.'

'Prince Faraj is greeting his father,' Farida framed with slightly raised brows.

Zoe coloured, wondering if her familiar use of Raj's name had offended. 'I didn't know he was a prince,' she said ruefully. 'He said he was nobody of any importance.'

Farida startled her by loosing a spontaneous giggle and turned, clearly translating Zoe's statement for the benefit of their companions. Much laughter ensued.

'The Prince was teasing you. He is the son of our King.'

Zoe's eyes widened to their fullest extent and she gulped. '*He's* the bad-boy Prince?' she exclaimed before she could think better of utilising that label.

'The bad boy?' Farida winced at that definition. 'No, I don't think so. He is my husband's best friend and he took a dangerous risk coming here to see us. '

'Oh…' Zoe noticed that Farida didn't risk translating her comment about Raj being a bad boy and resolved to be much more careful about what she said. According to Raj these people had had nothing to do with her kidnapping and they had looked after her well while she was unable to look after herself. She didn't want to slight them.

After all, she knew next to nothing about Raj, had merely read that tag for him on a website she had visited, which had contained the information that he had been sent into exile years ago for displeasing his father, the King.

'Risk?' she found herself pressing, taut with curiosity. 'What did he risk?'

'That is for his telling—*if* he has the opportunity,' Farida said evasively. 'But do not forget that the Prince is the King's *only* son, his only child in fact. He was born to the King's third wife when he had almost given up hope of having an heir.'

Zoe nodded circumspectly, unwilling to invite another polite snub and swallowing back questions that she was certain no one, least of all Farida, would wish to answer. Stupid man, she thought in exasperation. Why on earth hadn't he told her who he really was? It was not as though she could have guessed that he was of royal blood. She felt wrong-footed, however, and, recalling how she had assaulted him, gritted her teeth. It was his own fault though: he shouldn't have crept up on her like that.

An adorable toddler nudged her elbow in pursuit of a piece of apple and Zoe handed it over, waving her hand soothingly at Farida, who rebuked the little girl.

'No, my daughter must learn good manners,' Farida asserted.

'What's her name?' Zoe asked as the toddler planted herself in her lap and looked up at her with eyes like milk-chocolate buttons, set beneath a wealth of wavy black hair.

Farida relaxed a little then, and talked about her three children.

Accompanied by Omar, Raj strode into his cousin's tent where his father awaited him, seated by the fire.

'I thought I would find you here,' his father informed him with a look of considerable satisfaction. 'You are grown tall, my son. You have become a man while you have been away. Omar, you may leave. We will talk later.'

Raj's appraisal of the older man was slower and filled with concern because he could see that Tahir had aged. It was eight years since he had seen his father in the flesh. His parent had been in his fifties when Raj was born twenty-eight years earlier and the agility that had distinguished Tahir then had melted away. From a distance, Raj had watched his father's slow, painful passage to the tent, recognising that the rheumatoid arthritis, which had struck his parent in his sixties, now gripped him hard in spite of the many medical interventions that had been staged. He was still spry but very thin and stiff, the lines on his bearded face more deeply indented, but his dark eyes remained as bright and full of snapping intelligence as ever.

'Sit down, Raj,' the King instructed. 'We have much to discuss but little time in which to do it.'

Raj folded lithely down opposite and waited patiently while the server ritually prepared the coffee from a graceful metal pot with a very long spout. He took the tiny cup in his right hand, his long brown fingers rigid as he waited for one of his father's characteristic tirades to break over his head. Tahir was an authoritarian parent and had become even more abrasive and critical after the death of his third wife, Raj's mother. Sadly, that had been the period when Raj had been most in need of comfort and understanding and, instead of receiving that support, Raj had been sent to a military school where he was unmercifully bullied and beaten up. From the instant Raj had left school, he and his father had had a difficult relationship.

'I knew that Omar would run to you for help. He never had a thought in his head that you didn't put there first,' Tahir remarked fondly. 'We will not discuss the past, Raj. That would lead us back to dissension.'

'I'm sorry, but this woman…' Raj began even though he knew the interruption was rude, because he was so keen to find out why his father had acted as he had and had risked an enormous scandal simply to take his brother down a peg or two.

'You never did have a patient bone in your body.' Tahir sighed. 'Have sufficient respect to listen first. I want you home, Raj, back where you belong, as my heir.'

Raj was stunned. For a split second he actually gaped at the older man, his brilliant dark eyes shimmering with astonishment and consternation.

His father moved a hand in a commanding gesture to demand his continuing silence. 'I will admit no regrets. I will make no apologies. But had I not sent you away, my foolish brother would never have plotted to take your place,' he pointed out grimly. 'For eight years I have watched you from afar, working for Maraban, loyally doing your best to advance our country's best interests. Your heart is still with our people, which is as it should be.'

Raj compressed his lips and gazed down into his coffee, dumbfounded by the very first accolade he had ever received from his strict and demanding parent.

'Do you want to come home? Do you wish to stand as the Crown Prince of Maraban again?'

A great wash of longing surged through Raj and his shoulders went stiff with the force of having to hold back those seething emotions. He swallowed hard. 'I do,' he breathed hoarsely.

'Of course, my generosity must come at a price,' the King assured him stiffly.

Unsurprised by that stricture, Raj breathed in deep and slow. 'I don't care who I marry now,' he declared in a driven undertone, hoping that that was the price his father planned to offer him. 'That element of my life is no longer of such overriding importance to me.'

'So, no longer a romantic,' his father remarked with visible relief. 'That is good. A romantic king would be too soft for the throne. And it is too late to turn you into a soldier. But your marriage… On that score I cannot compromise.'

'I understand,' Raj conceded flatly, shaking his hand to indicate that he did not want another cup of coffee, for any appetite for it had vanished. Sight unseen, some bride of good birth would be chosen for him and he and his bride would have to make a practical marriage. It would be a compromise, a challenge. Well, he was used to challenges even if he wasn't very good at compromises, he acknowledged grimly. But he would have to learn, and fast, because it was unlikely he would have much in common with the bride chosen for him.

'I should thank Hakem for bringing the Fotakis

girl to my attention because I didn't even know she existed,' the King mused with unconcealed satisfaction. 'I was outraged when I realised what my brother was planning to do. I was even more outraged when I realised that I had no choice but to approach Fotakis himself…the man who stole the beautiful Azra from me. But he has given his permission.'

Only then registering what the older man was proposing, Raj threw his head back in shock. 'You're expecting me to marry *Zoe*?'

'And to do it right now, today. I brought the palace *imam* with me,' his father told him bluntly. 'This marriage would be your sign of good faith, your pledge to me that from now on you will act as a sensible son. Marry her and I promise you that nothing will stand in your path.'

'Zoe wants to go home!' Raj pointed out incredulously. 'She will not want to marry me.'

'Her grandfather has given his permission,' the King pointed out with a frown of bewilderment. 'A prince for a prince and a bridegroom less than half Hakem's age, you make an acceptable substitute in Fotakis's eyes. You have no choice in this, Raj. The girl is too great a prize to surrender, a huge gift to our people. No more popular bride than Azra's granddaughter could be found for you. We will have a big state wedding to follow. I believe she is as beautiful as her grandmother. You should be pleased.'

Raj compressed his lips on the reality that his father was insane. He talked as though women still dutifully and happily married the husbands picked by their most senior male relative. But even in Maraban those days were long gone. It was now only men of his father's venerable age who still expected the right to tell their offspring who they should marry.

'Zoe wants to go home,' he repeated steadily.

'You have two hours to persuade her otherwise. I have already prepared an announcement to be made from the palace,' the King told him solemnly. 'Their Prince has come home and done his duty at last.'

'Zoe was expecting to divorce Hakem within a few months,' Raj reminded his parent tautly.

'Yes, you can let her go once the fuss has died down. You can choose your own second wife,' Tahir informed him with the lofty air of a man bestowing a gift on the undeserving. 'I won't interfere, although there is one exception to that rule. That whore, Nabila…you cannot bring her into the family under any circumstances.'

At the mention of that name accompanied by that offensive term, Raj lost every scrap of colour, his eyes lowering, his expression cloaked by his spiky black lashes, for he had just learned that his father *knew* what had happened eight years earlier between his son and his first love. Discomfiture filled him to overflowing but the meeting, Raj recognised by that final warning, was over. He vaulted upright with something less than his usual grace. 'There is no risk of that development. I've not seen her in many years,' he revealed stiffly.

'Go and get ready for your wedding,' his father urged, clearly not accepting the possibility that Zoe might refuse to marry him. 'And send Omar in!'

Having had her breakfast, Zoe was ushered into another tent and left there alone. She checked her watch, shifted her feet, frustrated that she didn't know what the cause of the hold-up was. When Raj entered, she spun fully round to face him and then she froze, remembering uneasily that he was a prince and that she had not treated him as she should've done. But then that was *his* fault, she reminded herself, lifting her chin again. He looked tense, the smooth chiselled bones of his face taut beneath his bronzed skin, his dark deep-set eyes curiously intent on her.

'I thought you were in a hurry to leave,' she reminded him, wondering why even that scrutiny could heat her up inside her skin as if she were being slowly roasted. He made her feel hot and bothered and uncomfortable and if that was sexual attraction, well, then she wanted no part of it. Those physical reactions were affecting her ability to behave like a rational being.

'My father spoke to me *and*...our situation has changed,' Raj admitted, half turning towards the open doorway, avoiding a more direct look at her, lest he lose his concentration.

Any man would've looked though, he assured himself. Her beautiful hair was restrained in a long braid but he still remembered that silken veil unbound. Her shapely legs were exposed by a short skirt. The matching top in soft pastels moulded to her rounded breasts, and on her feet were the most ridiculously impractical heels he had ever seen a woman wear in the desert. Of course, she hadn't known that she would be waking up in the desert, but those towering heels, which still only contrived to lift her a couple of inches in height, were downright dangerous. At the same time, there was something absurdly feminine and cute about those tiny glittery sandals with their plethora of straps. He dragged in a deep breath, gritted his white even teeth. *Cute?* What was he thinking?

That it was safer to look at her feet than her breasts or her legs when his body was behaving as though it belonged to a sex-starved teenager. Since when had he been unable to control his libido? He could not recall ever having that problem before.

Zoe was very stiff, picking up on the undertones

in the atmosphere while reading the physical tension he was putting out in waves. '*Our* situation?' she queried, surprised by that designation.

'Ours,' Raj emphasised. 'I don't know how much you know about me.'

'Well, you told me that you were nobody of any importance but Farida told me the truth—that you are the King's son,' Zoe countered in a tone of reproof. 'I also know that you were sent into exile.'

'Eight years ago,' Raj clarified sombrely. 'I refused to marry the woman my father chose for me because I was in love with someone else. There were other factors but essentially that is what caused my long estrangement from my father. You may not be aware of it but in my world a son is expected to be obedient and, to be fair to my father, I was a rebel from day one.'

More than a little disconcerted by that very personal explanation of his troubled relationship with his parent, Zoe coloured, her green eyes clinging to his brooding dark features and the fluctuating emotions he was striving to hide; only those expressive eyes of his continually gave him away, glimmering and glittering, alive with all the passion he struggled to contain. Unwilling fascination gripped her and she gave way to her curiosity. 'What happened with the woman you loved? Did you marry her?'

'No, she cheated on me,' Raj admitted flatly.

'I'm sorry,' she muttered automatically, wishing she hadn't asked.

'You don't need to apologise. It happened a long time ago when I was still young, trusting and naïve. I am not the same man now,' Raj parried wryly.

Because that woman had broken his heart, Zoe registered, recalling her sister, Winnie's heartbreak when she had had to leave the man she loved, after discovering that he was married. Zoe had never experienced anything that intense and she wasn't sure she wanted to either. But then she had never had a boyfriend. After the attempted rape she had fortunately escaped, she had feared and avoided men. She had had one or two male friends at university who had stayed close to her for a while to test her boundaries, hoping she would warm up to them but it hadn't happened. She had stayed apart and untouched and was much inclined to think that that was the best way to live. Without risk, without hurt, without disappointed hopes and unrealistic dreams of some fantasy happy future.

'You said "our" situation,' she reminded him, keen to steer the conversation out of deep waters. 'What did you mean by that?'

'My father has offered me a most unexpected suggestion,' Raj framed with care, brilliant dark eyes locked to her heart-shaped face and the eyes bright as emeralds against her porcelain pale skin.

The contrast was breathtaking. 'He has asked me to come home and take my place as his heir again.'

'My goodness, that's wonderful news! I mean…' Zoe hesitated '…if *that* is what you want?'

'I want to come home with my whole heart. This is the first time I have been home in eight years,' Raj admitted harshly, his sincerity bitingly obvious. 'But unfortunately, the King's proposition came with a key stipulation attached. My father has asked me to take Hakem's place as your bridegroom and marry you.'

Zoe blinked several times and continued to stare at him, her heart thumping rapidly enough that it seemed to thunder in her ears. 'But…but why? That's a crazy suggestion!'

'Not if you consider who you are,' Raj pointed out with a wry twist of his wide sensual mouth. 'Half our population are originally from your grandmother's country and they were most resentful when my father and their Banian Princess failed to marry at the same time as the two states allied to become one. As a result, the royal family does not reflect the origins of both countries. If the King's son were to marry Princess Azra's granddaughter, it would be very popular with our people. Principally, *that* is why my father wants us to marry.'

'But I never even met Azra. She died before

I was born,' Zoe argued. 'It's just an accident of birth.'

'No, it is your heritage and a vital and proud heritage to those who remember the Princess and a country that now only exists as part of Maraban,' Raj contradicted. 'I should also mention that your grandfather and my father have been in touch—I should imagine only through an intermediary—and this suggestion that you remain here to marry me instead has been discussed by them.'

'Good heavens… Grandad *knows* about all this?' Zoe gasped, already shaken by Raj's serious respect for her ancestry, which was, she realised finally, far more valued in Maraban than it would ever be anywhere else.

'Your grandfather is agreeable to the exchange of bridegrooms,' Raj delivered.

Zoe turned slowly pale with anger. 'But what about me? What about what *I* want?' she demanded starkly.

'That is why I am here…*asking*,' Raj stressed sardonically. 'Your grandfather and my father are quite happy to believe that only their consent is required. I am not that foolish.'

Her anger drained away again. 'Thank goodness, someone here has some sense,' she mumbled.

'You were willing to marry Hakem sight unseen,' Raj reminded her.

Zoe's knees felt weak and she flopped down on

a cushioned seat as if her breath had been stolen from her. She was at a crossroads. 'That's different, that was before all this happened and I realised Hakem had abandoned his wife for me and stuff like that,' she argued uncomfortably. 'It was a mistake to agree. Now I just want to forget all this nonsense and go home again.'

'But I am asking you to stay here and marry me,' Raj stated with precision. 'And it is an entirely selfish request.'

Taken aback at that confession, Zoe tilted her head back to look up at him. 'Is it?'

'Yes. It would mean the end of my exile and my estrangement from my father,' Raj pointed out grittily. 'And not only that, my marriage to Azra's granddaughter would delight my people as well. What is in it for you other than the acquisition of an entirely useless title, I don't know, but it would at least be as much as you would have received from my uncle. I can also promise to treat you as well as he would have. He is a decent man, regrettably poisoned by his pointless need to compete with my father.'

What is in it for you? Zoe appreciated his honesty with regard to the advantages to him should he marry her. Even so, her understanding of his position did nothing to stop her brain from whirling with wild indecision. She had been ready to go home and give up on her quest for greater independence but now Raj was offering her another option. Yet somehow marrying him struck her as a far more intimidating prospect than marrying a much older man, who had sworn he would treat her like a daughter. Raj was so much younger, more aggressive, more virile… Her brain ran out of descriptive words as she glanced warily at him.

He was so poised in his long white buttoned tunic, a black cloak folded back over his broad shoulders, his lean, darkly handsome face grave and cool while he awaited her answer, those glorious dark-as-the-devil eyes gleaming with an impatience he was too polite and intelligent to voice. A positive reply would mean a lot to him. She understood that, she really did. She also still yearned for the opportunity to live an independent life, unfettered by the expectations of her family. But most of all, she wanted to prove herself to herself and she wanted to be strong without leaning on anyone else for support. Even less did she want to run home with her tail between her legs and disappoint her grandfather as well.

'What would it take to win your agreement?' Raj pressed, the skilled negotiator that he was breaking cover.

Zoe coloured as if he had turned a spotlight on her and dropped her head. 'Well, I don't know what your expectations would be but I can assure you now that I wouldn't want sex. I'm not into sex. It's something I can live without, but *you*?'

That he couldn't even look at her without thinking about sex was a truth Raj decided he needed to keep to himself. Overpowering curiosity assailed him at the same time. What had put her off sex? One bad experience? An assault? Those were not questions he could ask and he suppressed the urge to probe deeper even as he winced inwardly from the upfront immediate rejection she was handing him. She didn't want sex with *him*. He had never met with that kind of rejection before and he pushed away that awareness, deeming it arrogant and ultimately unimportant in the greater scheme of events.

'I can offer you the exact same marital agreement that persuaded you that you could marry my uncle,' Raj broke in to insist with measured cool.

Zoe tossed her head back in surprise. Little tendrils of white-blonde hair were beginning to cling to her damp brow because she was feeling too warm even in the shade of the tent. Probably because even talking about sex set her cheeks on fire with self-consciousness, but she knew that she had to be frank with him. There was no other way and no room for any misunderstandings if she was candid from the outset. It shook her to acknowledge that she was seriously considering the marriage he was suggesting, for it was unlike her to take a risk. And Raj, her sixth sense warned, would be a risk.

'Unfortunately, you're not old enough to treat me like a daughter!' she told him ruefully.

'But I am old enough not to put pressure on a woman, who doesn't want me, for sex,' Raj retorted without hesitation. 'I appreciate that you would have to take that guarantee on trust but it *is* the truth. I have never had to put that kind of pressure on a woman and I never will.'

'OK,' Zoe mumbled, feeling that they had done the topic of sex and not having it to death. 'I admit that I would like to stay in Maraban and explore a little of my heritage.'

'I could make that possible,' Raj told her.

'Where would we live?'

'In the palace, which is, I must admit, a little dated,' Raj acknowledged, choosing to understate the case because he himself considered his surroundings immaterial as long as the basics were in place.

His father, unhappily, had a great reverence for history and it had proved a major battle to persuade Tahir to allow even modern bathrooms and cooking facilities to be constructed in the ancient building. Guests were lodged in one of the very contemporary villas built within the palace compound to provide convenient accommodation for visitors while preserving his father's privacy.

'I could live with dated,' Zoe muttered uneasily. 'I'm really not very fussy. My sisters and I lived in some real dives before we met our grandfather a couple of years ago and he invited us to move into a property that he owns in London.'

'The palace is not a dive,' Raj murmured with reluctant amusement. 'To sum up, you are prepared to consider my proposal?'

'Thinking about it, wondering if I can trust you.' That admission slid off the end of Zoe's tongue before she could snatch it back and her face flamed with guilt.

'I keep my word...*always*,' Raj proclaimed with pride, dark eyes aglow with conviction. 'You have nothing to fear from me. You would be doing me a very great favour. The last thing I would do is harm you. In fact, if you do this for me, I will protect you from anything and anyone who would seek to harm you.'

He was gorgeous, she thought helplessly, standing there so straight and tall and emotional, *so* very *emotional*. She had never met a man who teemed with so much emotion that he couldn't hide it. She had never met a man she could read so clearly. Reluctant hope, growing excitement and the first seeds of satisfaction brimmed in his volatile gaze. She couldn't take her eyes off his, could still hear the faint echo of his fervent promise to protect her from all threats.

'We would still be able to get a divorce after a few months?' Zoe checked anxiously.

'Of course. We would not want to find ourselves stuck with each other for ever!' Raj quipped with sudden amusement.

And for the very first time in a man's presence, Zoe felt slighted by honesty. She scolded herself for being oversensitive. Naturally, he wouldn't want to stay married for good to a woman he didn't love and neither would she wish to stay with him, would she? He was simply voicing the facts of their agreement.

'Then…' Zoe rose to her feet, suddenly pale with the stress of the occasion and the big decision she was making for herself without consulting her sisters, who probably would've voiced very loud objections '… I will agree to marry you and I can only hope that it brings you the advantages that you believe it will.'

Raj took a sudden step forward and raised his arms and then let them fall again as he stepped back. 'Forgive me, I almost touched you but I am sure you prefer not to be touched.'

'I do.' But Zoe was lying. He had been about to sweep her up in his arms and hug her and she was disappointed that he had recalled her rules and gone back into retreat. He was passionate, a little impulsive, she suspected, the sort of guy who occasionally in the grip of strong feeling would act first, think later. She would have liked the hug, the physical non-sexual contact, the very warmth and reassurance of it, but it was better that he respected her boundaries, she told herself urgently. 'So when will this marriage take place?'

'Today.'

'Today?' she exclaimed in soaring disbelief.

'My father does not trust me enough to allow me to return to the palace without immediate proof that I have changed my ways,' Raj told her grimly. 'This marriage will provide that proof. He brought the palace *imam* here with him.'

'We're getting married here...*now*?' she prompted incredulously. 'What on earth am I going to wear?'

'My father leaves nothing to chance. I would suspect that his wife has brought appropriate clothing for you.'

'Which wife?' she prompted curiously.

'He only has one wife still living. My mother died when I was nine and her predecessor died about ten years ago. The Queen, his first wife, is called Ayshah,' Raj proffered. 'She is pleasant enough.'

Zoe breathed in deep and slow. She was going to marry Raj and make a go of her life all on her own. She would stay in Maraban for several months and there would be no more panic attacks. She would pick up some of the language, learn the history and find out about her grandmother's culture. It would be an adventure, a glorious adventure, she told herself firmly while watching Raj stand by the doorway, quite unconscious of her appraisal. He smiled with sudden brilliance. And gorgeous wasn't quite a strong enough word for him at that moment…

CHAPTER FOUR

'MY FATHER TELLS me that the King is arranging a state wedding to take place in two weeks' time and for that you can wear a Western wedding gown,' Farida informed Zoe in a discreet whisper. 'The King wants to make the most of your entry into the family.'

Apprehensive enough about the wedding about to take place, Zoe could have done without the news that there was to be a second, which would be a public spectacle. Such an event lay so far outside her comfort zone that even thinking about it made her feel dizzy. But she squashed that sensation. Baby steps, she told herself soothingly. She would cope by dealing with one thing at a time, and fretting about the future would only wind her up. Right at that moment it was sufficient to accept that she was about to legally marry a man she had only met for the first time that day.

Marrying Raj's uncle, however, she would have been doing the same, she reminded herself wryly, and at least Raj came without previous attachments such as wives, children and grandchildren. Yes, she had definitely dodged a bullet in not marrying Hakem. Raj was single and refreshingly honest. He had admitted that he had once suffered panic attacks too. He had even admitted to defying his father over the woman he loved and subsequently discovering that she had cheated on him, which must have been a huge disillusionment. Most men that Zoe came across would have concealed such unhappy and revealing facts. That Raj had been so frank had impressed her.

Surrounded by fussing tribeswomen presided over by the elderly Queen Ayshah, who sat in the corner, entirely dressed in black, barking out instructions, Zoe studied her reflection in the tall mirror. She was so heavily clothed in layers and jewellery that she was amazed she could move. A beaten gold headdress covered her brow, a veil covering most of her hair, weighty gold earrings dangling from her ears, hung there by thread. She had very narrowly sidestepped having her ear lobes pierced there and then and she had Farida to thank for tactfully suggesting thread be used to attach the earrings instead. More primitive gold necklaces clanked and shifted round her neck with every movement while rich and elaborate henna swirls adorned her hands and her feet. What remained of her was enveloped in a white kaftan covered in richly beaded and colourful embroidery. Below that were several gossamer-fine silk layers, all of which rejoiced in buttons running down the back. Getting undressed again promised to be a challenge, she thought ruefully.

She had insisted on doing her own make-up though, having run her eyes over her companions, already festooned in their glad rags and best jewellery for the wedding, their faces over-rouged, their eyelids bright blue. Only Farida had gone for the subtle approach. Zoe had used more cosmetics than she normally did and had gone heavy on the eye liner when urged to do so but at least there was nothing theatrical about the end result.

'My wedding celebrations lasted a week,' Farida told her.

'A *week*?' Zoe gasped.

'But yours will only last the afternoon. The King does not wish to spend the night here. The state wedding celebration parties will go on longer, I expect,' Omar's wife chattered. 'Everyone loves these events because they get to see family and friends, but this has been arranged so quickly that it is a very small and quiet wedding—but the jewellery Raj has given you is magnificent.'

'What jewellery?' Zoe whispered.

'Everything you're wearing comes from the royal house. Traditionally, the jewellery is your wedding gift.'

'The King must've brought that with him as well,' Zoe muttered.

'Yes, you were getting married today whether you wanted to or not!' Farida laughed. 'But who could say no to Raj?'

Zoe could feel her face heat and was grateful when the sound of music outside the tent sent all the women to the doorway. She followed them and glanced out to see some sort of ceremonial dance being performed with much waving of swords and cracking of whips. Men leapt over the campfire, competing in feats of daring that made her flinch and at one point close her eyes. A moment later, she was ushered out in an excited procession into another larger tent filled with people. She was led up to the front where a venerable older man appeared to bestow some sort of blessing on her and gave a long speech before handing her a ring. Farida showed her which finger to put it on. In the middle of the speech, she finally glimpsed Raj, resplendent in a sapphire-blue silk tunic, tied with a sash, his lean, darkly handsome features very serious. She tried and failed to catch his eye.

Another, even older man spoke more briefly and then moved forward to flourish a pen over a long piece of parchment, which he duly signed. In fact, several people signed the parchment and then she in turn was urged forward to sign as well, before being led away again without a word or a look exchanged with Raj.

'And now we party!' Farida whispered teasingly in her ear.

'You mean…that's it *done*? We're married now?' Zoe exclaimed in wonderment.

'As soon as you signed the marriage contract, it was done. I would've translated for you but I didn't want to risk offending the King by speaking during the ceremony,' the lithe brunette confided. 'You are now the Crown Princess of Maraban.'

'And I don't feel the slightest bit different!' Zoe confided with amusement, reckoning that her grandfather would be sorry to have missed the ceremony but she assumed he would be attending the state wedding, which was to follow. Her sisters would have to come as well and she smiled at the prospect as Farida guided her into yet another tent full of chattering women where music was starting up in the background.

Introduction after introduction was made and plate after plate of food was brought. There were no men present. Farida explained that the reception after the state wedding would not be segregated but that rural weddings were of a more conservative ilk. Zoe sipped mint tea and watched the festivities as the dancing began. Married, she kept on thinking; she couldn't believe it. But she wasn't really married, she reminded herself wryly, not truly married because she and Raj were not going to live together as a married couple. She wondered how he was feeling. Was he wishing she were his ex-love, who had let him down? Or did the significance of the actual marriage escape him because he was not in love with his bride? Or, more likely, was he simply happy that he was back in Maraban and accepted by his father again?

At one point, Zoe drifted off in spite of the noise and liveliness surrounding her and wakened only when Farida discreetly pressed her hand. She blinked in bemusement, for an instant not even knowing where she was. Darkness had fallen beyond the tent and it was quieter now, only a couple of women dancing, the rest gathered in chattering groups. Slowly her brain fell back into step and she suppressed a sigh, murmuring an apology to Farida for her drowsiness.

'Your body is probably still working on ridding you of the sleeping drug you were given at the palace. Our doctor said it would be a couple of days before you fully recovered from that. I am so sorry that that happened to you,' the other woman said sincerely.

'You were involved in it against your will…not your responsibility,' Zoe pointed out gently.

'And sadly, the instigator will only be celebrating the reality that he has regained his son,' Farida murmured ruefully.

The last piece of the puzzle fell into place for Zoe and her eyebrows shot up in surprise as she finally appreciated that only Raj's father could have had her kidnapped and remained safe from punishment of any kind. That was why Raj had remained silent about the identity of the perpetrator; that was why he had seemed to feel partially responsible for her ordeal. Clearly the King had been determined to prevent his brother, Hakem, from marrying her.

'It is time for you to retire,' Farida told her, reacting to a signal from Queen Ayshah, who raised her hand and gave her a meaningful look.

That the old lady was still going strong while she felt weary embarrassed Zoe. She lumbered upright, feeling like an elephant in her cumbersome layers of clothing, hoping it was cooler outside than it was inside. But that was a false hope, she recognised when the humid air beyond the tent closed in around her and she was forced to trek across the sand in her wildly unsuitable shoes that dug in at every step. A camel was led in front of her and made to lie down. Farida instructed her to climb into the saddle, which, weighted down as she was by fabric and jewellery, was no easy task, but at last the deed was accomplished and the animal scrambled up again and swayed across the sands in the moonlight, accompanied by whoops from the women crowded round her and with the aid of the herdsman with his very modern torch.

'It is symbolic,' Farida explained. 'Queen Ayshah stands in your mother's place and she is sending you to your bridegroom.'

Zoe rather thought it was more as if she were a parcel to be delivered, although thank heaven, she reflected with a choked giggle, Raj wouldn't be expecting to *unwrap* the parcel. She slid more than she dismounted from the camel and picked herself up off the sand, thinking fondly that she was having an even more exciting wedding day than either of her sisters had enjoyed while wondering when her mobile phone would be returned to her so that she could bring her siblings up to date with events.

She almost staggered into the tent lit by lanterns that awaited her and there she froze in consternation. A large bed confronted her and it dawned on her at last that this was her wedding night, which she was expected to spend in close proximity to her new husband. She wasn't going to get her own tent this time or even her own bed because she was supposed to *share* the bed. In silence she pulled a face because she hadn't anticipated that, although she knew that she should've done.

After all, her agreement with Raj that their marriage would be platonic was a private matter that neither of them was likely to discuss with anyone beyond their immediate family. Grateful when the women retreated again she sank down on the bottom of the low divan and breathed in deep while she waited for Raj to arrive. My goodness, she was getting so hot. She straightened and walked into the primitive bathroom that had been erected alongside and clearly in haste for their comfort. A mirror sat propped up on a chest and piece by piece she removed the heavy gold jewellery and set it on the chest along with the veil.

At that point she heard shouts and catcalls outside and she scrambled up to return to the main tent just in time to see Raj striding in and covering the door again with obvious relief. 'Everyone gets overexcited at weddings,' he said wryly, studying her with fixed intensity.

Colour mantled her cheeks, self-consciousness reclaiming her as she hovered. 'Perhaps they're also celebrating the fact that their Prince is home again,' she suggested.

'It is possible,' Raj fielded with quiet assurance.

He wore confidence like invisible armour and she envied him that gift, wondering how he could ever have suffered the ignominy of panic attacks. He had the innate calm of a man comfortable in his own skin yet, from what little she had already learned, his past was littered with drama and disappointment. Yet he had overcome those realities and moved on, much as she wished to do.

'Do you know where my clothes are? Are they

still back at the house I was taken from?' she asked uncomfortably.

'I will enquire for you in the morning,' Raj murmured smoothly.

'I don't even have a toothbrush!' Zoe protested, falling back on trivialities rather than dealing with her insecurities over the situation she was in.

'I will give you one,' Raj informed her in a tone of finality.

Zoe swallowed hard on a burst of angry exasperation. Was she supposed to go to bed naked with all her make-up on? It wasn't his fault that she had been separated from her luggage, she told herself urgently, and she shouldn't take her ire out on him. Deal with it, she instructed herself, and she went back into the bathroom and removed the ornate kaftan before beginning to undo the buttons of the layers beneath. Arms aching, perspiration dampening her face, she stalked back uneasily into the bedroom. Raj was on his phone, black eyes skimming to her instantly. He cast the phone down and studied her enquiringly.

'I'm afraid I need your help with all these buttons,' she framed in considerable embarrassment. 'I don't want to tear anything…'

'No, that would indeed be embarrassing,' Raj conceded. 'It would look as though I ripped the shifts off you.'

Breathing fast, Zoe spun round, presenting him

with her slender back. 'I just don't get why it has all those buttons in an absolutely inaccessible place!'

'Because you are not supposed to take it off by yourself,' Raj informed her softly, a faint tremor racking her as she felt the gentle pressure of his fingers against her back as he undid the buttons, because a man had never got quite that close to her before and that he should be undressing her, even though it was at her request, was still a challenge. 'Your bridegroom is supposed to remove the three shifts slowly and seductively. It is a cultural tradition.'

'Oh…' Zoe gasped and then as the ramifications set in, *'Oh,'* she said again.

'You will have Ayshah to thank for the shifts because I don't think most brides bother with this particular tradition these days,' Raj told her huskily, skimming the first shift down her arms and letting it drop to the rug beneath her bare feet before embarking on the next set of buttons. 'That is a shame.'

'Is it? A bridal version of the dance of the seven veils…or whatever?' Zoe heard herself wittering on nervously, cringing even as the words escaped her.

Raj rolled his eyes and gritted his even white teeth because peeling her out of the silk shifts was testing his self-control. Her skin glimmered through the gossamer-fine tissue like the most lustrous of pearls and that close the sweet scent of her, of roses and almonds, was unbelievably feminine and alluring. Raj tugged down the second shift and let it fall before stepping away, carefully not looking at what would now be an enhanced view of her body because he did not require that encouragement.

Bemused, Zoe spun round, registering that he had stopped and walked away. 'I don't want to sleep in this one,' she muttered uncomfortably. 'These shifts are precious to your stepmother. They were put on me with a care that implied they were made of solid gold.'

'She is not my stepmother,' Raj incised curtly. 'She is my father's first wife.'

'Right… OK,' Zoe framed, registering that she had hit a tender spot with that designation, but very much out of her depth when it came to labelling or understanding the doubtless complex relations created in a family consisting of more than one wife. 'But what am I to sleep in?'

Raj was forced to look at her and the image locked him in place. She was so clueless he swallowed hard on impatient words. She might as well have been standing there naked for the thin material hid very little. The pert little swells of her small breasts were obvious, not to mention the intriguing tea-rose colour of her prominent nipples and the pale curls at the apex of her thighs. Raj sucked in a sustaining breath, hot and hard as hell. 'I will get you something of mine,' he asserted, rather hoarse in tone, his dark deep voice roughening the vowel sounds.

'I'm sorry I'm being such a pain,' Zoe mumbled uneasily as Raj dragged out a leather holdall and opened it to rummage through it.

'I didn't bring much because I didn't think I'd be staying long.' Raj sighed, finally extracting a T-shirt and a pair of boxers for her use.

Zoe grabbed the garments with alacrity and spun round beside him. 'Just undo the last ones, please, and I'll be out of your hair,' she promised.

Raj suppressed a groan, his attention locking on the sweet curvaceous swell of her bottom. Presented with the delights of her in reality his imagination could take flight with ease and he ached with arousal. He grappled with the buttons, no longer deft, indeed all fingers and thumbs as he thought of laying her down on the bed and teaching her the consequences of teasing a man. But even as he thought of such a thing, he was grimly amused by it because he knew she was quite unaware of the effect she was having on him and that he would never touch a woman who had stated so clearly that she did not want to be touched. In fact, he had never been with a woman less aware of her seductive power over a man and, while at first he had found that absence of flirtation and flattery refreshing, now, suddenly, he was finding that innocence of hers a huge challenge.

'Now you can go and take it off and get changed,' Raj informed her thickly.

Zoe turned back to him, catching the harsh edge to his voice and looking up at him to see the dark glow of his eyes accentuated by the flare of colour over his high cheekbones. 'Raj…what's wrong?' she questioned helplessly.

'How honest can I be?' Raj asked.

'I want you to feel that you can always be honest with me. In fact, that's very important to me.'

'Even if it embarrasses you?' Raj prompted.

'Even if it embarrasses me,' Zoe confirmed without hesitation.

'You are half naked and very beautiful,' Raj breathed huskily. 'I have sworn not to touch you but I am still a man and you tempt me. You can still trust me to keep my word but I would be grateful if you…' He fell silent because Zoe had already backed into the bathroom, her face as startled and as red as fire.

Only ten feet from him, separated only by tent walls, Zoe looked at herself in the last shift and she burned all over with mortification. She'd had no idea quite how sheer the shifts were because at no stage had she seen her reflection in them in the mirror. Half naked seemed like an understatement when she was showing everything she had got! Shame and chagrin enveloped her. He had said she tempted him. Dear heaven, did he think her display had been deliberate? No, surely not. She peeled off the last shift, laid it carefully to one side and stepped into the shower, hoping it would cool her off. She didn't want to go back into the bedroom and look him in the eye again.

Cold water drenched her and she stood there as long as she could bear it, before, shivering, she got out and grabbed a towel off the pile. He had been frank with her and she was glad of that, she reflected ruefully. If they were to live in close proximity, she would have to be more careful, more *aware* in a way she had never had to be before. His T-shirt fell past her knees and she put on the boxers, although they struck her as overkill.

'Zoe?' Raj murmured quietly.

She peered into the bedroom and he handed her a toiletries bag.

When even her teeth were clean, she *had* to return to the bedroom but she looked nowhere near him as she crossed to the bed and climbed in straight away.

Raj went for a long cooling shower and tried to remember when he had last had sex. It had been weeks and weeks. He should make more effort in that department, he told himself firmly. Had he formed the habit of regular sex, he was convinced he wouldn't have been so tempted by Zoe. But then, it had been years since he had enjoyed regular sex, he acknowledged ruefully. These days he had occasional one-night stands and he never spent the night because he had discovered that spending too long with the same woman only encouraged the kind of entanglements and expectations that made him feel trapped. 'One and done', he called his routine. He didn't do relationships, he didn't do girlfriends, he didn't do dates. Nabila had sent him flying off such a conventional path.

But Zoe, the wife he could not touch, he was learning to his cost, was a whole new ball game…

Zoe peered out from under the sheet as Raj strode across the tent, his long, lean, powerful body clad only in boxers. Her eyes widened, drawn by the flex of steel-hard muscle across his bronzed torso. He was a work of art, she thought numbly, barely able to accept that such a thought could be hers and that for the first time ever she was admiring the male body, which had until that moment inspired her only with fear. But then Raj was something else, Raj somehow fell into a totally different category and she didn't understand how that was or even why. Yet he was one of the most masculine men she had ever met. Everything about Raj from his innate poise to the rough stubble now darkening his jaw line and the well-honed strength of his physique screamed male. She closed her eyes tight, blanked her mind and slowly, inexorably fell asleep.

The nightmare that assailed her was an old familiar one. She was sprawled on the floor of an old hut, sneering thugs surrounding her while another cut off her clothes with a terrifyingly sharp knife. She was trapped. Shouting or screaming only earned her another punch and she was already in a great deal of pain because one arm and a leg were broken and, she believed, several ribs. She could barely see out of her swollen eyes but there was nothing wrong with her ears and she could hear every one of the filthy, perverted things they were threatening to do to her. She was petrified, lapsing in and out of consciousness, fighting the sickening effects of concussion…and outside a thunderstorm was crashing and banging like extra evidence that she had been plunged into a living hell.

'It's OK…it's OK,' a vaguely familiar voice was assuring her and she clung to that voice like a drowning swimmer, letting it pull her fully out of the bad dream.

'No,' she croaked in a shaken whisper. 'I'll never be OK again.'

Outside the thunder crashed deafeningly loud and she flinched and gasped, registering that there really was a storm outside, just as there had been the night she had almost been gang-raped. 'I don't like storms,' she muttered, clutching at his warm, solid body for support.

'You were having a nightmare, moaning, shouting for help. I tried to wake you up,' Raj admitted. 'But it took a long time to bring you out of it.'

'The storm confused me, probably woke me in the end… There was a storm in the nightmare too…except it wasn't really a nightmare, it was something that happened to me…but it's been years since I dreamt about it,' Zoe framed shakily. 'I'm sorry.'

'You don't need to apologise. We can't police our dreams,' Raj dismissed, leaning away from her to light the lantern by the bed.

Her anxious eyes widened at the sight of him because being in bed with a half-naked man felt so very alien to her. And Raj was all male as he stretched, that fantasy V-shape flexing across his lower rock-hard abdomen as he shifted to reach for a glass of water and handed it to her.

Colour rising, Zoe gulped down water as if she were suffering from dehydration. She didn't like the way her brain was spewing random sexual thoughts at her. It was scary being that close to Raj and wanting to touch him. *Touch* him? What insanity was attacking her? Since when had she wanted to touch a man? Yet all of a sudden she could imagine *touching* Raj, smoothing a hand over that satin-smooth golden skin laid down over muscle. She sat up and put the glass down just before another deafening crash of thunder boomed and it sent her careening into the shelter and security he offered like a homing pigeon.

Raj had never before found it a problem to have an armful of fragrant woman in his arms. But when the woman was Zoe, it was a major problem. He had heard her shouting for help and saying, 'No, *please…*' over and over again and a kind of unholy rage had gripped him that someone so small and defenceless had been driven to begging, her fear and desperation palpable. Only it became complicated when she got too close to him and his body reacted against his will. He was so hard he dared not leave the bed for fear that she would notice and get scared that he couldn't be trusted. But he was not made of stone.

He closed his arms round her, murmuring soothing things in his own language, doing his best to resist urges that he felt should shame him. 'Were you raped?' he asked in a roughened undertone.

Zoe flinched, her slender body trembling in his hold, and she looked up at him. 'No. I was lucky. I was beaten up but I was rescued before it got that far.'

Raj's level black brows lifted. *'Lucky?'* he derided, not only stunned by what she had told him, but also feeling honoured that she had trustingly bestowed such a terrifying secret on him.

And Zoe laughed and spontaneously smiled. 'Yes, very lucky. I'm a survivor.'

That glorious, utterly unexpected smile was more than Raj could withstand. Zoe looked up into eyes as bright as liquid starlight and marvelled at the beauty of them. He lowered his head and claimed her soft pink mouth with his.

The thunder boomed beyond the tent. Lightning strafed the ground, lighting up the walls, but Zoe didn't hear or notice any of that because there was a kind of magic in Raj's kiss and it was like no kiss she had ever had before. And yes, she had had kisses before, had tried several times at university to get into the spirit without succumbing to the terror of getting out of her depth with some guy who might then get angry and refuse to listen to her protests. When Raj slid his tongue between her parted lips, an insistent heat she had never felt before flared between her thighs. His hands stroked through her hair and she felt her breasts swell and her nipples tighten and tingle. The warmth of his skin and the weight of him against her led to the discovery that her body liked those masculine aspects of him. Even more did she appreciate the aromatic smell of him, an insanely attractive combination of musky male and designer cologne, which tugged at something very basic inside her.

His tongue brushed hers and withdrew, leaving her aching for more, every nerve ending on fire.

And then he set her back from him and dragged in a shuddering breath while still looking at her as though she were the only woman in the universe, a gift of his that yanked at her heart strings. 'I'm sorry,' he breathed in a raw undertone. 'I broke my promise not to touch you.'

'Do you see me running or screaming?' Zoe demanded, shaken by his sudden withdrawal while her body was still humming and pulsing like an unfamiliar entity.

Raj's slightly swollen and very sensual mouth compressed, dark eyes glittering with angry regret. 'I will not make excuses for myself but I assure you that *this* will not happen again. Go to sleep, Zoe. You are safe.'

Since she didn't have much choice, Zoe turned away and snaked back to her own side of the bed, defensively turning her back to him. She had only herself to blame for the way she felt, she thought unhappily. She had told him she wasn't interested in sex, had shown him her fear and, in return, he had sworn not to touch her. Naturally he was angry that he had broken that pledge. Sixth sense told her that Raj didn't usually break promises and probably didn't think much of those who did. But he had warned her earlier that he found her attractive and their current circumstances of false intimacy and mutual dependence only made resistance more difficult.

But for the first time in her life, Zoe had *wanted* a man and she knew that she wasn't likely to forget the crazy buzz of excitement that he had unleashed inside her. She, she reflected in mortification, had been more tempted than he was because he had quickly called a halt.

And what had she wanted to do?

To her eternal shame, she had wanted to snatch him back and *make* him keep on kissing her and, not only that, in the back of her mind she had been well aware that she craved more than that. Somehow, and she really didn't know how or when it had happened, she was finally ready to *try* sex, to experiment, but there was no room for sex in their agreement, particularly in a marriage destined to last only a few months.

When she wakened in the morning, Raj was gone, but one of her suitcases sat in a prominent position near the bed. With a smile of relief, she got up and went to open it before going to freshen up. Clad in light cotton trousers and a pink top, teamed with glittery sandals, she found breakfast awaiting her on her return. She was really hungry and tucked in with appetite, although she was no fan of the yogurt drink included, reckoning it was probably one of those healthy options that she rarely enjoyed.

She walked out of the tent and an explosion of utterly unexpected colour greeted her. A field of flowers stretched before her and she walked in amongst the colourful blooms in wonderment at such a floral display in so seemingly inhospitable a landscape.

'Zoe…stay where you are!' Raj shouted at her, incensed to see her outside and unprotected and wandering with a toddler's absence of caution.

'What on earth—?' she began, glancing up from the pink, purple and mauve blooms she was studying as she crouched.

But Raj, black curls shining, was sheathed in jeans and a T-shirt and already striding towards her, careless of the flowers he crushed beneath his feet, clearly untouched by the beauty of the scene. He scooped her up bodily in his arms, exclaiming in Arabic. 'And what the hell are you wearing on your feet?' he then demanded incredulously.

'Sandals!' she snapped. 'You stood on the flowers of an *asphodelus fistulosus* and it was the only *one* in this mass of bugloss.'

'There are scorpions and snakes, lying in the shade below the flowers!' Raj bit out, startling her. 'Here you wear only proper footwear that protects you.'

'Oh… OK.' Zoe nodded, recognising concern and superior knowledge when she saw it. 'I didn't know…but the flowers were so beautiful.'

Raj carried her back to the tent, thinking that he would never forget that first glimpse of her in that sea of flowers, white-blonde hair falling to her waist and glittering like highly polished platinum in the sunlight, and those huge green eyes blinking dazedly up at him as he lifted her, full of shock and incomprehension of the risk she had taken. He had trod on pretty flowers and it had bothered her. She was sensitive, also possibly a little ditzy to walk out thoughtlessly into what could be a very hostile environment. But it was his duty to take care of her, watch over her, his job to protect. And the enormity of such a responsibility sat heavy on his shoulders for an instant because he had never been responsible for another human being before.

Nor did he want to be responsible, he told himself staunchly. He would take care of her to the best of his ability without ever forgetting that she was not *truly* his wife and he refused to think of her as such. Zoe was a short-term prospect, not a keeper. He would be ice, he would remain impervious to her charms. He was not about to complicate things by getting too involved with her. He had hard limits and he would observe them, retaining softer feelings, if he could even experience such emotions again, for his future *real* wife. There would be none to waste on Zoe, even if she looked adorable posed amidst flowers. What an asinine thought that was! He surely had more sense than that, enough intelligence to keep his distance, he instructed himself bitterly; he had learned his lesson with Nabila.

Innocent didn't mean she was a virgin. He would never believe a woman's word on that score again! Cute didn't mean trustworthy. Nabila had lied like a trooper and he had not recognised her deceit. Adorable definitely didn't mean loveable. Cute and adorable were words that should never feature in his vocabulary because caring about the wrong woman hurt like hell and he wasn't revisiting that mistake for anybody!

CHAPTER FIVE

WITHIN AN HOUR a brief flight in the helicopter returned them to the palace.

Zoe walked through an ancient porticoed entrance and instantly felt as though she had been transported into another world and another time. An awe-inspiring giant hallway full of pillars and elaborately tiled walls greeted her as well as a wealth of fawning servants, some of whom were in actual tears welcoming Raj back to his home. Brushing off their blandishments with palpable embarrassment, Raj hurried her on into the building while a cohort of attentive staff fell in behind them.

'My father has placed us in the oldest part of the palace, which is…unfortunate,' he told her in a clipped undertone. 'It is, however, where the Crown Prince always has his apartments, so I cannot fault him for following tradition.'

'Why's it unfortunate, then?' she queried uneasily, even while her eyes fled continually to her surroundings. She was enthralled by the exotic quality of the internal courtyard gardens she espied from the stairs and the fabulous views out over the desert, not to mention the stonework, the domed roofs and the stern palace guards, dressed as though they had stepped out of a medieval painting, armed with swords and great curved knives. The palace was everything she had dreamt of when first coming to Maraban but far more grand and mysterious than she had naïvely expected.

'Only one bedroom has been prepared for us,' Raj breathed curtly, his strong jaw line clenching. 'It will be difficult to give you privacy.'

'We'll manage,' Zoe told him with an insouciance she could not have contemplated before meeting him in the flesh. She knew in her very bones that she could trust Raj, believed that he would never try to force her into anything, but when she pondered that conviction, she was challenged to understand why she had such faith in him. He'd shown her empathy, tenderness, kindness the night before, she reminded herself ruefully.

'That is very generous of you but not strictly within our agreement,' Raj pointed out, refusing to be soothed.

'Can't be helped,' Zoe murmured, breathless from trying to keep up with his long stride as he traversed long corridors at speed and mounted flights of stone stairs with lithe ease. 'This is a very large building.'

'But *not* modernised,' Raj retorted grimly, throwing wide a door before a hovering servant could reach for it and guiding her into a simply vast room in which a bed hunched apologetically in one corner.

'Plenty of space though!' Zoe carolled like Job's comforter.

The remainder of her cases were already parked along with the one that had travelled out to the desert encampment. A maid glided up and tilted one suggestively, looking eager to unpack, while Raj stalked across the huge Persian rug, like a jungle predator at bay looking for something else to complain about.

A connecting room, she quickly learned, contained cavernous wardrobes.

'This suite was last occupied by my father fifty-odd years ago,' Raj informed her grimly. 'You can tell.'

'You didn't use these rooms when you were younger?'

'No. Before my marriage I was expected to live in my father's household.'

Zoe passed on into a ridiculously gigantic bathroom with a great domed roof studded with star tiles. The bathroom fittings huddled somewhat pathetically against the walls. 'It just needs more furniture,' she told Raj with determined cheer. 'We could have one of those fainting couches in the middle and I could lie there like Cleopatra eating grapes.'

His starlit eyes focused on her without warning, an intensity within that look that made something quiver and burn low in her pelvis. *'Naked?'*

'Whatever turns you on,' Zoe mumbled, face burning, outclassed in her attempt to be lighthearted and dropping her head even while she pictured herself lying there naked for Raj's enjoyment. A ridiculous fantasy, she scolded herself, for there would be nothing particularly sexy or seductive about her very small curves on display.

'I have staff to introduce you to now,' Raj announced, biting back the comment that seeing her naked in any circumstances would work a treat for him. There would be no flirtation between them, he instructed himself harshly, no foolishness.

'Staff?' she exclaimed in dismay.

'Principally my PR team, but you will have your own PA to keep you well informed of events. My father has made certain requests. He would like you to give an interview to our leading newspaper.'

Zoe had frozen. 'An…*interview*?' she yelped in dismay.

'Saying how you feel about arriving in your grandmother's country and being on the brink of a state wedding. My team will advise you and remain with you during it. There is also a fashion stylist, who will recommend a suitable wedding dress and new clothes.'

'I brought a wedding dress and an entire wardrobe with me,' she informed him helpfully.

'It would be distasteful to me were you to wear the dress you purchased for the marriage you planned to make to my uncle,' Raj delivered succinctly. 'You will wear nothing bought for that purpose.'

Zoe just couldn't see why it should matter what she wore. 'Don't you think you're being too particular?'

Raj settled hard black eyes on her, startling her. 'No. I know what I like. I know what I *don't* like. The concept of you wearing anything chosen with another man in mind offends me.'

Zoe sucked in a sustaining breath, deciding that he was more sensitive to her past history than she had appreciated. She returned to supervising the maid hanging her clothes because it seemed safer to keep her head down.

'You will be kept very busy over the next few days choosing wedding apparel,' Raj informed her from the doorway.

'Can I use your phone for a few minutes?' Zoe asked abruptly. 'Mine needs charging and I want to catch up with my sisters and my grandfather.'

'Of course.' Raj dug out his phone, cleared the password and handed it to her. 'I will see you later.'

And then, just like that, he was gone and she was staring at the space where he had been, all black silky curls with his dark, devastatingly beautiful face taut and uninformative. She had wanted him to stay with her, had wanted *more*. For a charged moment, she couldn't cope with seeing that large gap between reasonable expectation and sheer idiocy for, naturally, Raj wasn't planning to hover over her like a protective and loving spouse because he wasn't really her husband in the truest sense of the word. No, he was genuinely offering her what she had told herself she needed and craved: an independent life in which they would live separate in mind and body. So why did that sensible arrangement now seem much less inviting? Why did his attitude currently feel like something of a rejection? She shook off that strange notion and told herself to stop overthinking everything before she drove herself mad.

Her grandfather was delighted to hear from her and eager to be assured that Raj was treating her properly, while adding that he would be arriving for the wedding, the fierce pride in his voice as he mentioned 'state' wedding so strong that it made her roll her eyes and swallow back a sigh. Winnie and Vivi were far less accepting of the change of bridegroom.

'He's a lot younger than the oldie,' Vivi warned her worriedly. 'Make sure he doesn't try to get too friendly because he may have a different agenda.'

And when Zoe protested about how kind and considerate Raj had been so far, Winnie snorted. 'He's a prince, a future king—obviously he'll be full of himself. And I looked him up online...he's incredibly good-looking. Watch out for him trying to change the terms of your agreement.'

But when Zoe went to bed that night there was no sign of Raj being full of himself or looking to change the terms of anything. He had joined her earlier for dinner out in their private courtyard, a space shaded by towering and somewhat neglected trees and shrubs, and he had then excused himself to work. She had been measured up for a new wardrobe, had looked at length at designer dresses on a screen and had stated her preferences. By the end of the day she was too exhausted to stay awake, wondering where Raj was.

Raj worked late into the night before bedding down on the sofa in his office. It was the safe option. A vision of Zoe naked troubled his rest and at four in the morning he was on his phone trying to find out what a fainting couch was; for some reason he was determined to buy one regardless of cost. He groaned out loud at the conflict tearing at him. He didn't want to get involved. He didn't want to have sex with her...except when his resistance was at a low ebb. Why the hell would he buy a fainting couch for her to pose on? He found a purple velvet one hung with tassels and pictured her with a driven exhalation of breath before he thumped the cushion beneath his head. No couch, no flirtation, no sex, no intimacy whatsoever, he reminded himself grimly.

'Well, I couldn't say much for the accommodation,' Vivi remarked with a decided sniff.

Zoe bit back a tart response because her sister had been making critical comments ever since she had arrived the night before and it was starting to annoy her. 'It's very comfortable and Raj says I can take furniture from any of the unused rooms in the palace or buy new stuff, but contemporary wouldn't really work in surroundings like these. I haven't had time yet to change anything with all this wedding craziness going on.'

'That monster bathroom is just ridiculous,' Vivi opined snarkily.

'Raj's father wouldn't agree to any structural alterations when the bathrooms first went in. As far as he can, the King wants to preserve the palace as it was when he took the throne and I can understand that. It's a very old and historic building and he feels more like the custodian for future generations than the owner who has a free hand,' Zoe pointed out.

'You've got more confident…that's clear and I definitely approve of that,' her eldest sister, Winnie, said warmly. 'Here you are giving interviews and the like. I never thought I'd see the day.'

'Oh, the interview was easy,' Zoe carolled. 'Raj's PR team headed off any too personal questions for me and advised me on what to wear and all the rest of it.'

'But you picked your own wedding gown,' Winnie said knowingly, scrutinising the tiny glittering figure of her youngest sister. The dress was an elegant sleeved sheath with a modest neckline. Elaborate embroidery sewn with crystals and pearls adorned the lightweight tulle and it was the perfect fit for her petite frame. 'It's very chic.'

'Oh, stop changing the subject, Winnie,' Vivi cut in curtly, keen to cut through the chit-chat to what she believed was truly important, which was *protecting* Zoe. 'You know that you're as worried as I am. We *talked* about it last night.'

'And we're not going to talk about it any more,' Winnie declared, throwing her fiery sibling a pleading look. 'It was Zoe's decision to do this and the deed is done. They're already married.'

'With *one* bedroom in a palace the size of a small city!' Vivi interrupted worriedly, seriously suspicious of that development. 'How's she going to fight off a guy twice her size?'

Zoe paled at the tenor of the conversation. 'I

won't have to fight him off. Raj sleeps elsewhere. We haven't had to share a bed since that first night I told you about, and that was kind of unavoidable and he apologised for it.'

'Raj is smooth, sophisticated, *predatory*,' Vivi outlined in condemnation, finally speaking her mind, for she had taken one look at Raj in all his good-looking, silkily soft-spoken glory and seen him as a major threat to the terrifyingly innocent and fragile little sister she loved. How could such a very handsome and wealthy man *not* be predatory? Zoe's near rape had almost destroyed her and Vivi didn't want her sister plunged into any situation that could threaten her peace of mind. 'I would imagine he is never stuck for the right word in a difficult situation.'

'He's not predatory,' Zoe argued with distaste. 'He's been kind. He's courteous and considerate and that's all we need right now.'

'Leave it, Vivi,' Winnie said ruefully. 'All you're doing is putting more pressure on her.'

Zoe's hand shook a little as she reapplied her lipstick. She was furious that Vivi had called Raj predatory after only meeting him for an hour over the formal dinner that had been staged the night before. Stam Fotakis, her grandfather, had been grudgingly impressed by Raj, pointing out to her with satisfaction that, unlike her sisters' husbands, Raj had never been tagged a womaniser.

Diamonds flashed with every movement of her body. Raj had sent her jewel cases containing a tiara, a necklace and earrings. She didn't know whether they were family heirlooms or bought specially for her use and she hadn't had the chance to ask him because she had barely seen Raj since their move to the palace two weeks earlier. He joined her for dinner every evening but his manner was formal and distant and she didn't know how to break through that façade.

And although she had tried to penetrate that barrier to establish a friendlier vibe, Raj remained resolutely detached and very, *very* polite. His attitude frustrated the hell out of her. She didn't know what the matter with him was or what was travelling through his brain. The warmer, milder, more approachable side of Raj had vanished as though it had never been.

Although she could have had no suspicion of the fact, Raj's attitude was frustrating his royal parent even more.

'Any normal man would want to *keep* her!' King Tahir was proclaiming to his stony-faced son.

'I have no intention of keeping Zoe as a wife,' Raj asserted quietly. 'You knew that going into this.'

'She's a beautiful, gentle girl. Everyone who has met her has talked highly of her. She could be a tremendous asset to you with her personality and ancestry,' his father fumed. '*Why* are you sleeping in your office with a beautiful wife in your bed? Have you forgotten how to woo a woman?'

The obstinacy that ran through Raj like a steel backbone flared and he gritted his teeth. 'She agreed to a fake marriage and I will abide by that agreement as I will abide by the one I made with you.'

The King paced the floor and silence fell. It was the silence of unresolved differences and residual bitterness that most often distinguished meetings between father and son. It took effort for the older man to persist. 'I loved your mother. I *know* she was unhappy as my wife but I loved her very much and the mode of her death devastated me,' he bit out harshly. 'I have to live with my regrets and my mistakes but I still remain grateful for the time I had with her.'

Raj swallowed hard, unable even to look at his father and utterly taken aback by that confession. He had never realised that his father actually loved his mother but he did recall that, after her passing, the older man had lived like a hermit for over a year. Not guilt so much as grief, Raj adjusted now, his view of the past softening the trauma of loss just a little.

Ironically, even appreciating that could not lift his gloom because there was nothing to celebrate when marrying a very beautiful woman who appealed to him on every level but who would ultimately leave him. His mother had left him by taking her own life, Nabila had left him through betrayal of all that he held dear. But then, hadn't he *agreed* that Zoe would ultimately leave him? Hard cheekbones colouring at that timely recollection, he reminded himself that he was in control of events and walking the path he had chosen. By the time Zoe walked out of his life again, he would surely be glad to reclaim his freedom.

The state wedding was so official and serious that Zoe's face ached with her set and determined smile. Being the cynosure of all eyes was taxing for her, but she wouldn't let herself dwell on that reality because she was well aware that all brides were subject to close scrutiny. Instead she reminded herself that she was lucky enough to have her grandfather, her sisters and their husbands with her for support. Sadly, the formality of the event had persuaded her sisters that their young children were better left at home and she suppressed a sigh. Winnie's son, Teddy, was a very lively little boy and her toddler daughter was full of mischief while as for Vivi's twin boys, sitting still for any length of time was a massive challenge for them, but Zoe was still disappointed not to have had some time with her nephews and niece because she had always adored children and had grieved over the truth that she was unlikely to have any of her own.

Yet her recognition of her attraction to Raj and her enjoyment of that amazing kiss had made her think that just maybe there was hope for her in the future. Maybe some day, after all, she would be able to have a relationship with a man like any normal woman, and if that happened then she just might have children of her own to love and care for eventually. More than anything else, what she had learned about herself since arriving in Maraban had convinced her that staying in her grandmother's country was the very best thing she could do to steer herself back into the land of the living. There was a whole world out there waiting to be discovered and for the first time in years she was filled with hope and optimism.

In the short term, however, she acknowledged wryly, there was the marrying, the constant smiling and the solemn bridegroom to contend with at their reception. If a smile had cracked Raj's face once she must not have been around to see it. A half-smile would play about the corner of his full sensual lips in the most infuriatingly tantalising way and she would watch and watch those lean, darkly beautiful features of his, but the real thing never quite made it, even for the authorised wedding photographs, which had proved to be an exercise in rigid formality.

Yet everywhere in Raj's radius, a virtual party was in swing, his return to being Crown Prince clearly a development that was celebrated by the many important guests attending, who ranged from visiting royal connections to business tycoons, top diplomats and local VIPs. His popularity was undeniable, although he was quick to dampen comments that tactlessly suggested that some day he would take Maraban forward in a different way from his father. Zoe sat through a lot of business talk before escaping back in the direction of her sisters.

She had already done her stint with Queen Ayshah, who had employed Farida as a translator and had embarrassed the other young woman greatly by insisting on passing on her convictions of what it took to be a good royal wife. A feminist would have had a field day with those rules, Zoe reflected with strong amusement, but then the elderly Queen had grown up in a different world where a woman's happiness and even her life could be utterly dependent on retaining her husband's favour. Thankfully, Raj would have no such power over her, Zoe thought fondly as she took a detour towards the cloakroom before approaching Winnie and Vivi.

In the big anteroom surrounding the cloakroom, a tall, slender woman rose from a chair and addressed her. 'Your Royal Highness?' she murmured with modestly evasive eyes. 'May I have a word?'

Zoe looked up into one of the most beautiful faces she had ever seen: a flawless oval graced by almond-shaped brown eyes with remarkable lashes, a classic slim nose and a pouty full mouth. The woman wore a sophisticated silk suit, tailored with precision to show off her well-formed figure and falling to her ankles while still toeing the line of local mores on modest dress. The pale golden hue of the outfit set off her glowing olive colouring and her wealth of tumbling black wavy hair to perfection.

'I am Nabila Sulaman,' she revealed in a very quiet voice. 'I was Raj's first girlfriend and, as I'm sure you're aware, it ended badly between us.'

Thoroughly disconcerted by that introduction, Zoe merely gave an uncertain nod while her mind raced to understand why the wretched woman would want to approach her.

'I run one of your grandfather's construction firms and he brought me here with his party of business people. I would definitely not have received an invite on my own behalf,' Nabila admitted, startling Zoe even more with that freely offered information. 'I'm very much a career woman and I don't want past mistakes to taint my future now that I've returned to Maraban to work. My parents suffered a great deal over my short-lived relationship with Raj. My father is a diplomat but he has been continually passed over for promotion since I blotted my copybook with the royal family. I am speaking to you now because a lot of time has passed since then and I was *hoping* that you could persuade Raj to bury the hatchet.'

Zoe winced at that bold suggestion. 'I'm sorry but I don't think I'm the right person to intercede for you. I don't interfere with Raj's life and he doesn't interfere with mine.'

'How very modern he must have become,' Nabila remarked with a dismissive toss of her beautiful head and an amused smile. 'Well, I think you should know that I'm in charge of the Josias project as CEO of Major Holdings, and that Raj and I will be working together in the near future. Please make him aware of that. I'm leaving now.'

'But Raj is here. You could speak to him yourself,' Zoe pointed out.

'No. I don't want to put him in an awkward position and surprise him in front of an audience,' Nabila declared with assurance. 'We haven't seen each other since we broke up.'

'Oh…' Bemused, Zoe watched the poised brunette walk away again and she entered the cloakroom with a lot on her mind. Nabila was gorgeous, clever and successful and had once been the woman Raj loved and wanted to marry, Zoe reflected ruefully. Loved and wanted to marry *a long time ago*. Eight years back, she reminded herself, practically pre-history in date. But even though that was her mindset she still headed straight for her grandfather to check out his opinion of the brunette.

'Nabila Sulaman? She's one tough cookie, a real go-getter,' Stam opined. 'Had to be to get so far in the construction field. She's Raj's ex?' Her grandfather grimaced. 'I wouldn't have included her in my party if I'd been aware of that.'

'Oh, it doesn't bother me,' Zoe hastened to proclaim just as her sisters joined them and then, of course, the entirety of her short conversation with Nabila had to be recounted.

'She's got some brass neck!' Vivi declared. 'I wish I'd been with you. Didn't you learn anything from us growing up?'

Zoe blinked and studied her sibling's exasperated expression. 'What do you mean?'

'You don't tangle with an ex. You certainly don't give her any information… I mean, what you were thinking of, telling her that you and Raj don't interfere in each other's lives?' Vivi demanded ruefully. 'How normal does that sound? You *want* the ex to think you're the love match of the century.'

'Put a sock in it, Vivi,' Winnie cut in. 'Zoe doesn't have to pretend if she doesn't want to. It's a marriage of convenience and both of them know and accept that. It's not personal for them the way it was for you and me.'

Zoe had lost colour. No, it was *not* personal, she repeated staunchly to herself, because, unlike her sisters and their husbands, Zoe had had no prior relationship with Raj before their marriage. Yet even in acknowledging that truth she was taken aback by the revelation that she would have liked to have scratched Nabila's beautiful eyes out because Nabila had *hurt* Raj. A long time ago, she reminded herself afresh, and he was perfectly capable of looking out for himself.

When the festivities were almost at an end, Zoe went to change into more comfortable clothing for their journey. They were to be out of the public eye for two weeks and she couldn't wait to reclaim some privacy. Apparently, the royal family owned a very comfortable villa by the Gulf on the Banian side of Maraban, and Raj had already promised to show her the beauties of her grandmother's birthplace, which was greener and less arid in landscape. She pulled on a light skirt and T-shirt, teaming them with a pair of glitzy high sandals, one of the many, many pairs she harboured in her wardrobe but had never previously worn. She had a serious shoe fetish and knew it.

'We're fortunate to be making so early an escape,' Raj remarked, sliding into the limo beside her, a lean, lithe figure in jeans and a shirt, his black curls tousled as though he had changed out of his wedding finery in as much of a hurry as her. 'If my father wasn't so eager to pack us off on a honeymoon, the celebrations would have lasted all week.'

'Farida mentioned that weddings usually last for days here, but then it was our *second* time round the block,' she pointed out before pressing on, doing what her conscience told her she had to do, which was to warn Raj that he would be working with his ex on some project that she didn't recall the name of. 'I met your ex-girlfriend, Nabila, at the reception.'

Raj's arrogant head turned, a frown building, his lean, darkly handsome face forbidding. 'That is not possible. She would not have been invited. Nabila is a common name in Maraban.'

'Apparently she came in my grandfather's party of guests,' Zoe persisted. 'She's the CEO of some company called Major Holdings and she asked me to warn you that you would be working with her on some project.'

'The Josias hospital project.' Raj's intense dark eyes shimmered almost silver in the fading light. 'But I need no warning. I am not so sensitive,' he breathed with roughened emphasis.

And then he didn't say another word for what remained of the fairly lengthy journey that took them to the airport and a flight and, finally, a bumpy trip in a SUV. And, unfortunately that brooding silence told Zoe everything she didn't want to know or surmise about the exact level of Raj's sensitivity. He was like a pot of oil simmering on a fire but all emotion and reaction was rigidly suppressed by very strong self-control that acted like a lid. But knowing that, accepting that she hadn't a clue what he was thinking, didn't make Zoe feel any happier. For the first time with Raj, she felt very alone and isolated…

CHAPTER SIX

WITH DIFFICULTY, RAJ emerged from circuitous thoughts laced with outrage at the prospect of being exposed to Nabila's deceitful charm again and stepped out of the SUV. He expected to see the sprawling nineteen-twenties villa that his family had used as a holiday home since his childhood. He blinked in disbelief at the very much smaller new property that now stood in its place and signalled the army major in charge of their security to seek clarification of the mystery. A couple of minutes later he returned to Zoe's side.

'Apparently, my father had the old villa demolished several years ago because it was falling into disrepair and he thought it was too large to renovate,' Raj explained. 'It was built by your great-grandparents at a time when the Banian royal family had half a dozen daughters. My family used it rarely after your mother's father died. My father likes the sea but the Queen does not.'

Relieved that Raj was talking again, Zoe murmured, 'Did you come here much as a boy?'

'Often when I was very young with my parents. My mother loved it here.' His lean strong face tightened, his perfect bone structure pulling taut beneath his bronzed skin. 'I remember her skipping through the surf and laughing. No worries about etiquette or protocol or who might be watching and criticising her behaviour. She could be an ordinary woman here again and she loved it.'

'An *ordinary* woman?' Zoe queried, puzzled by that label.

Momentarily, Raj turned away to evade the question because he disliked talking about past traumas. In his experience a trouble shared was not a trouble halved and he preferred to gloss over such issues. Without skipping a beat, he deftly changed the subject. 'My father should have told me that there was a smaller property here now,' Raj breathed. 'As he only comes here alone, there may only be one bedroom.'

'Oh, let's not get into *that* debate again!' Zoe carolled with a comically exaggerated shudder that locked his eyes to her animated face. 'We're adults, we'll get by, even if you make me sleep on the floor!'

Her green eyes could dance like emeralds tumbling in sunlight, Raj noted abstractedly, settling a hand to her spine to guide her down the path because it was dark and she could hardly move in her high heels without stumbling on the stony surface beneath their feet. He had watched her throughout the day, had been forced to watch her teeter and sway and steady herself on furniture every time she lost her balance. She might continually wear high heels but had evidently not yet learned how to comfortably walk in them. The idea of her falling and hurting herself made him want to go into her wardrobe and *burn* every one of those preposterous shoes. It was an odd thought to have and he tagged it as such and frowned in bemusement.

'You know, I wouldn't do that.'

'You're not sleeping on the floor either!' Zoe warned him as they approached the well-lit front door. A lovely wrap-around veranda fronted the building and their protection team surged ahead of them to check that the house was safe. 'Where have you been spending the night since we got married?'

'My office.'

'Is there a bed there?'

Raj shrugged a broad shoulder. 'A sofa,' he admitted grudgingly.

Zoe gritted her teeth in annoyance. 'Are you *that* scared of me?'

Dark colour scored the hard, slanted lines of Raj's spectacular cheekbones and his stunning eyes flashed gold with angry disbelief. At that optimum moment the protection team reappeared to usher them inside. It didn't take long to explore the interior of the beach house. There was a surprisingly large contemporary ground-floor living area and a winding staircase led upstairs to a spacious bedroom and bathroom.

'There's no kitchen!' Zoe exclaimed abruptly, glancing out at the walled swimming pool beyond the patio doors. 'How are we supposed to eat here?'

'The staff stay in a new accommodation block built behind the hill and cater to our needs from there,' Raj told her. 'Meals will be delivered. It's not a very practical arrangement but my father enjoys his solitude.'

'I'm starving,' Zoe admitted.

'I will order a meal.'

'I'll go for a shower and change into something more comfortable,' Zoe said cheerfully.

She was halfway up the stairs when Raj spoke again. 'I am not scared of you, nor was I implying that you would choose to tempt me into breaking my promise,' he assured her levelly. 'But it annoys me that my father is making it so difficult for me to offer you the privacy I swore to give you.'

'And why *is* he doing that?' Zoe prompted, tipping her head to gaze down at him, her cheeks warm from his misapprehensions about her. No, she wouldn't ever set out to deliberately tempt him but she was painfully conscious that she wanted him to make some kind of move on her because she was keen to explore the way he made her feel. It was just sex, she told herself guiltily, sexual urges tugging at her hormones, and there was nothing more normal than that, she told herself in urgent addition, nothing to be ashamed of in such fantasies. It was simply her bad luck that she was married to an honourable male who believed in keeping his promises and not taking advantage. Luckily for her, she could not even imagine a scenario where she would tell him honestly how she felt and, for that reason, the humiliation of making a total fool of herself over him was unlikely.

In the meantime, all she could freely do was glory in the sheer physical beauty of Raj, his wonderful broad-shouldered, lean-hipped and long-legged physique that magnetically glued her attention to him, the dark deep-set eyes that were silver starlight when he stared up at her, his perfect golden features taut. Heaven knew, he was gorgeous and it was little wonder she was obsessed, she conceded ruefully. He had broken through her barriers, made her experience feelings she had never known she could feel, but he hadn't intended to do that and now she was stuck with the rules according to Raj, which had about as much give in them as steel bars.

'My father believes you could be my perfect

for ever wife. He's hoping for more than a pretend marriage from us and obviously he's doomed to disappointment,' Raj extended drily.

'Oh…' Deprived of speech by that piece of bluntness and stung by the assurance that she was safe for ever from being asked to entertain the idea of something *other* than a pretend marriage, Zoe sped on into the bedroom.

There was so much she didn't know about Raj, she reflected. All she had were the bare bones of his background and the fact that his first love had cheated on him. At least, she was assuming that Nabila had been his first love but, really, what did she know? Little more than was available on the Marabanian website about the royal family. And ignorance was *not* bliss. Raj had frozen and backed off the instant she'd asked about his mother. Nabila wasn't the only no-go zone; his mother clearly was as well. Zoe heaved a sigh as she showered, wondering what had made Raj quite so complex and reserved.

Raj glanced up from his laptop as Zoe reappeared downstairs, clad in some kind of pastel floaty dress that bared most of her shoulders and a slender length of shapely leg. Not even the most severe critic could have deemed the outfit provocative, but her pert little breasts shifted as she completed the last step and he went instantly hard, cursing his libido and the fierce desire he was holding back that was becoming harder and harder to contain. Most probably he would need her covered from head to toe not to be affected, he conceded wryly, and what good would that do when he had already seen her virtually naked and could summon up that mental image even faster? He clenched his teeth together, hating the sense of weakness she inflicted. It was weak to want what he knew he shouldn't have. He prided himself on being stronger and more intelligent than that.

Nabila had been enough of a mistake to scar a man for life, a warning that his judgement wasn't infallible, that people lied and cheated to get what they wanted or merely to make a good impression and cover up the less presentable parts of their character. But, at least, he no longer carried resentment where Nabila was concerned, he reflected absently. Time had healed his bitterness and maturity had taught him more about human nature. Even so, the very prospect of having to deal with Nabila in any form, most particularly in a professional capacity in the company of others, was deeply distasteful to him. It was even more offensive to him that Nabila had dared to approach his wife and introduce herself. That had been brazen and, although he knew that Nabila could be utterly brazen and calculating, he could not begin to understand why she had made such an inappropriate move.

'Wow…look at the food!' Zoe whispered in wonderment as she glimpsed the array of dishes spread across the low table in front of him. 'You should've started without me.'

'I do have *some* manners,' Raj told her huskily, amusement glimmering in his shrewd gaze.

'I never said you didn't,' she muttered in some embarrassment, lifting a plate to serve herself and watching him follow suit. 'But I did take ages in the shower.'

Raj could have done without that visual of her tiny, delicately curved body streaming with water. 'I had a shower before we left the palace.'

'I didn't have time and it was so warm in that car even with the air conditioning.' She sighed. 'So, I'm about to ask you to be straight with me on certain issues because if you aren't I could slip up and say something embarrassing to the wrong person,' she pointed out, trotting out the excuse she had come up with in the shower to make Raj talk about what he didn't want to talk about. 'Who was your mother?'

Raj tensed and swallowed hard. 'She was a nobody in the eyes of most. Ayshah and my father's second wife, Fairoz, were both royal princesses from neighbouring kingdoms and my father married them to make political alliances when he was in his early twenties. Since *he* did *his* duty in the marital line you can understand why he expected me to be willing to do the same eight years ago.'

'Yes, but he grew up during a very unsettled period of Maraban's history when there was constant war and strife. It was different for you because you didn't live through any of those wars or periods of deprivation,' Zoe told him calmly, her retentive memory of what she had read about Maraban's history ensuring that she had a clear picture of past events. 'Now tell me about your mother and why she was nobody in the eyes of others.'

'She was a commoner, a nurse. My father had heart surgery in his fifties and she looked after him in hospital.'

Zoe smiled in approval. 'So, it was a romance?'

'Well, no, for most of my life I assumed he simply took my mother as a third wife in the last-ditch hope that a much younger woman could give him a child,' Raj confided with a twist of his full sensual mouth. 'That was the perceived reality. It never occurred to me that he had fallen in love with her until he admitted that to me only a few days ago. Now I am shamed by my prejudice but, in my own defence, my mother was a very unhappy wife and I remember that too well.'

'Why was she unhappy?' Zoe pressed.

'Picture the situation, Zoe,' Raj urged with rueful emphasis. 'Two childless older wives of many years were suddenly challenged by a much younger new arrival and they didn't like it. They didn't think my mother was fit to breathe the same air as their husband and when she quickly fell pregnant, as they had failed to do, their resentment and jealousy turned to loathing. They bullied her cruelly and treated her like dirt. My father likes a quiet life in his household and he did not interfere between his wives. He ignored the problems.'

'I'm *so* sorry,' she murmured, registering that Raj must have been old enough to understand how his mother was being abused and that his troubled relationship with his father and Ayshah probably dated from that period.

'By the time I was nine years old, she was so depressed that she took her own life with an overdose. It happened here in the old original house. Perhaps that is also why my father had it demolished,' he admitted in a driven undertone. 'There, now you know the whole unhappy story of my childhood.'

Zoe reached for him, her small fingers spreading to grip his much larger hand in a natural gesture of sympathy, finger pads smoothing over the sleek brown skin. 'Thank you for telling me,' she whispered. 'I wouldn't have pushed so hard if I'd known it was a tragedy.'

'She was a wonderful, loving mother but it was many years before I could forgive her for leaving me,' Raj confessed in a rueful undertone.

'I have no memory of either of my parents. I was only a baby when they died in a car crash,' Zoe told him with regret. 'Cherish the memories you have, try and build a bridge with your father. Everybody needs family, Raj.'

'I prefer not to need *anyone.* Independence, in so far as it is possible, is safer. Do you want something sweet to finish?' Raj enquired in casual addition. 'There is a fridge hidden in that cupboard over there. The maid filled it with desserts.'

Listening to him, Zoe had lost much of her appetite, but she scrambled upright and fetched the desserts to serve, knowing that Raj would welcome that distraction. It seemed that she always, *always* put her foot in it with him. She should have been more patient, should have waited until he was willing to talk, instead of forcing the issue. Beating herself up for her nosiness soon led to her faking a yawn and saying she was going up to bed.

Raj worked on his laptop for an hour, giving Zoe time to fall asleep. He mounted the stairs as quietly as he knew how and then he saw her, lying on the bed in something diaphanous, the pool of light surrounding her veiling her entire body in soft gold. She looked up from her book, green eyes wide, little shoulders tensing, petite breasts pushing against the finest cotton to define the pointed tips and that was the moment that Raj finally lost the battle. Hunger surged through him with such power it virtually wiped out conscious thought. She was there, she was where he wanted her to be and, in that moment, she *was* irresistible.

Zoe was fiercely disconcerted when Raj simply stalked like a prowling jungle cat across the room and bent down to snatch her up into his arms. 'Raj?' she exclaimed uncertainly, all the breath from her body stolen by that action.

'I want you… I *burn* for you,' he breathed rawly. 'Tell me to put you down and I will walk away. I will not try to railroad you into anything you don't want.'

Zoe stared up into his silvered eyes and her entire body clenched while her heart pounded in her ears. 'I want you too,' she admitted breathlessly, barely able to credit that she had the nerve to admit that and yet if he could admit it, why shouldn't she?

As he cradled her in his arms, a faint shudder of relief racked his lean, powerful frame and he claimed her parted lips with so much passion he took her by storm. Head swimming, mouth swollen, she plunged her fingers into his silky black hair, revelling in the crisp luxuriance of his curls and holding him to her. There was no sense of fear, no sense of threat and she rejoiced in that freedom, pushing up into the heat of him as he brought her down on the bed. She yanked at his shirt as he reached for her nightdress, their combined movements ending up in a tangle.

'We're behaving like teenagers!' Raj rasped in disbelief, gazing down, nonetheless, at her flushed and lovely face with ferocious satisfaction. He had never craved anything as much as he craved her hands on his body and he leant back from her to pull his shirt up over his head and discard it.

Zoe looked up at him, secretly thinking that she was behaving like a teenager because her experience of men was probably about that level. She truly was a case of arrested development, cut off from normality at the age of twelve when everything to do with men and sex had frightened her into closing down that side of her nature. Now she wondered if she should warn him that she was a virgin, but wasn't there a strong chance that her inexperience would turn him off? Or, at least, make him pause to consider whether they should be having sex in the first place? She didn't want Raj to stop and ESP warned her that if cautious, logical Raj got in charge again, her desire to have sex for the first time could be thwarted.

Raj, however, chased away all her apprehensive thoughts simply by taking his shirt off. As he leant back over her to toss it away, his abdominal muscles flexed like steel girders and she gazed up at his superb bronzed torso with helpless appreciation. Heat flowered low in her pelvis, making her press her thighs together on the resulting ache. Exhilaration flooded her at the knowledge that she was finally feeling what other women felt when they desired intimacy with a man.

'I thought you didn't like sex,' Raj breathed in a driven undertone.

And then I met you.

But she wasn't going to frighten him off by telling him *that*, was she?

'It's time I tried again,' she muttered obliquely.

'I will endeavour not to disappoint you,' Raj growled, his lips ghosting in a whisper of a caress across her collarbone that made her shiver, lean brown hands tugging up the nightdress inch by inch, fingertips lightly glossing over her slender thighs and finally her narrow ribcage. The butterflies fluttering in her belly took flight.

The nightdress fell away and Zoe sat up to embark on his jeans. It might be her first time but she wasn't about to lie there like some petrified Victorian virgin and let him do everything, she told herself squarely. Her hands were shaking so much though that she could hardly get the zip down and he closed a steadying hand over hers, pressing her fingers against him before arching his hips to snake lithely out of his jeans. His boxers went with them and she stared at the evidence of his arousal and then, dry-mouthed, reached out to stroke him, her heart already racing as though she had run a marathon.

The instant she touched him, Raj tugged her up

against him with a hungry groan and crushed her mouth under his again, his tongue prying apart her lips and skating across the roof of her mouth before colliding with hers. Another burst of heat shot through her, tightening her muscles, and she shifted closer still, wanting the hard heat of him plastered to every inch of her. He was so passionate and she loved that passion, could feel it surging through his lean, powerful body to meet her own.

He laid her back and shaped her breasts with sensuous hands, smoothing, massaging, moulding, before dipping his head to catch a straining pink nipple in his mouth and swirl his tongue round the throbbing peak until her spine arched and a stifled gasp was torn from her. She was much more sensitive there than she had ever realised and little tingling thrills began to dart through her, trickling down into her pelvis to create a hot liquid pool between her thighs.

Her hips arched up of their own volition, her body controlling her responses, and all the time the nagging craving at the heart of her was building to an unbearable level and she was making little impatient sounds she couldn't quell. When he finally touched her where she most needed to be touched, her body jackknifed and a wild flood of sensation seized hold of her, provoking a cry from her lips. It was her very first climax and the sheer intensity of it took her by surprise.

Raj smiled down at her and kissed her even more hungrily. 'You are so receptive,' he husked.

Lying there dazed by the experience, Zoe reached up to explore him, palms spreading across his chest, captivated by the strength and heat of him before sliding lower to encounter a restraining hand.

'Not now,' Raj grated out. 'I'm too aroused and I need to be inside you. Are you protected?'

For a split second she didn't know what he was talking about and then comprehension sank in and she shook her head in an urgent negative. With a groan, Raj sprang off the bed naked and dug into his luggage, spilling out everything on the floor in wild disarray and then leafing through the tumbled garments to retrieve a wallet and extract a foil packet.

'I only have a few. I will need to buy more. I have not been with anyone recently and we must be careful.'

Warmed by his admission that he had had no recent lovers, Zoe frowned.

'Careful?' she queried.

Surprised by the question, Raj glanced at her. 'In our situation, a pregnancy would be a disaster… not that it's very likely. Look how many years it took my father to produce a child!' he urged wryly. 'For all I know a low sperm count runs in the royal genes.'

'But contraception is pretty much foolproof these days…surely?' Zoe pressed.

'Nothing's foolproof in that line. Accidents and surprises still happen,' Raj pointed out, coming back down on the bed with a smouldering look of hungry urgency silvering his stunning eyes. 'But it will *not* happen to us.'

Zoe reddened, disconcerted to find herself in the very act of picturing a little boy or girl with his spectacular dark eyes. Some day in the future, she promised herself, and most definitely she would become a mother with someone she had yet to meet. Raj would just be an experience she recalled with warmth, she told herself; nothing more, nothing less was due to the man who had rescued her from her fears.

She stretched up, winding her arms round his neck to draw him down to her and she kissed him, enjoying that freedom and that new confidence to do as she liked, and it all came from the reassuring, delightful discovery that Raj appeared to want her every bit as much as she wanted him.

He tugged at her lower lip with the edge of his teeth, sent his mouth travelling down the elegant line of her slender neck and that fast conversation was forgotten as another cycle of arousal claimed her. Her temperature rose, a fevered energy gripping her limbs as her heartbeat quickened and her breathing fractured.

Excitement quivered up from her pelvis when she felt him surge between her thighs, sliding into her inch by inch, sending the most exquisitely unexpected sensations sizzling through her.

'You're very small and tight,' Raj ground out breathlessly.

And then with a final shift of his lean hips he forged his passage and her whole body jerked with the pain of it and she cried out.

Raj stilled. 'What's wrong?'

Mortified that she had made a fuss, Zoe grimaced. 'It hurt more than I was expecting. It's my first time.'

As shock clenched Raj's lean, darkly handsome features and he began to withdraw from her, Zoe grabbed his shoulders. 'No, don't you dare stop now!' she told him. 'I've been waiting such a long time to experience this.'

The deed was already done, Raj rationalised, but anger was roaring through his taut body and it was only with difficulty that he swallowed it back because he didn't want to risk hurting her any more…even if she had chosen to have sex with him as though he was an adventurous new experience much like a day out behind the wheel of a supercar, he reflected wrathfully.

'Raj, please…don't make a fuss,' Zoe urged, studying him with huge green eyes that pleaded.

And Raj did what every nerve ending in his

body urged him to do and surged deeper into the welcome of her, a low growl of sensual pleasure wrenched from him. And from that point on, no further encouragement was required. A wondrous warmth began to rise low in her pelvis, building on the visceral ache for fulfilment, making her fingernails dig into his long smooth back as excitement seized her and held her fast. The feel of him over her, inside her, all around her sent rippling tremors of joy spiralling through her and when she hit the heights again, it was explosive.

In the aftermath she felt as though she were melting into the bed in a boneless state and the very last thing she needed then was Raj freeing himself from their entangled limbs and springing off the bed to breathe rawly, 'You've got some explaining to do. You *lied* to me!'

CHAPTER SEVEN

GRABBING THE SHEET to cover herself, Zoe hauled herself up against the tumbled pillows, watching Raj yank on his jeans. Going commando, she noticed, colour flaring in her face. It was as if her mind weren't her own any more. She couldn't take her eyes off his lithe bronzed body, couldn't concentrate.

'I didn't lie,' she reasoned stiffly.

'You *lied*,' Raj repeated wrathfully. 'You said it was time you tried sex *again* when clearly you had never had sex before—'

'Well, I may have blurred the edges of the truth a bit,' Zoe mumbled defensively.

'You lied and I detest dishonesty!' Raj shot back at her fiercely.

'So what?' Zoe fired back, her temper sparking in answer to his.' It was *my* decision to make—'

'And mine. I wouldn't have touched you had I known I would be the first!' Raj bit out curtly.

'But you chose to withhold that knowledge, which was unfair—'

'Oh, for goodness' sake…' Zoe thrust the blonde hair falling round her hot face back off her damp brow. 'It was just sex. Why are you making such a production out of it? We're consenting adults, neither of us is in another relationship.'

Raj skimmed scorching dark eyes to her. 'I don't do relationships.'

'Well, I'm afraid you're *stuck* in this one,' Zoe told him with unashamed satisfaction. 'You can't have it both ways, Raj. If you don't do relationships, then you should be quite happy to have had no-strings-attached sex.'

Dark colour scoring his superb cheekbones, Raj shot her a blistering look of derision and strode out of the room. She listened to his bare feet thumping down the wooden stairs and then the slam of the front door signifying his exit from the house. Switching out the lights, she got out of bed to walk over to the window and finally picked him out striding down onto the beach. Moonlight glimmered along the hard line of his broad shoulders and danced over his curls.

Mortification gripped Zoe, who was conscious she had said stuff she didn't actually believe to hit back at him because she had felt humiliated by his annoyance. It *had* been her decision to have him as her first lover, hadn't it? But she wasn't liberal enough to plan to have casual sex with anyone, even if she had made it sound as though she were. She had simply wanted that experience, had wanted *him*. Was that so bad? But it also felt wonderful to no longer fear the act of sex, to no longer feel that she was somehow less than other women and missing out on an experience that others enjoyed.

Uneasily aware then of the ache at the heart of her from that first experience, she went into the bathroom and ran herself a bath to soak in. She had messed up, brought sex into their platonic relationship…but, hey, hadn't Raj been the one to make the first move? Why hadn't she thrown that at him? It was *his* fault they had ended up in bed. Why, in his eyes, would it have been acceptable to become intimate if she had had more experience? How had it somehow become wrong because she had been inexperienced?

Throwing on a cotton wrap and stuffing her feet into flip-flops, Zoe left the house and trudged across the sand to where Raj was walking through the whispering surf.

Raj heard her approach. There was nothing stealthy about Zoe crossing sand. He breathed in deep and slow, rising above his angry discomfiture and the guilt she had inflicted him with.

'All right, I'm sorry I didn't tell you beforehand, but you're the one who dragged *me* into bed,' Zoe reminded him flatly, her face burning. 'Regrets now are a bit late in the day and they're not going to change anything.'

'In my culture a woman's purity is highly valued and respected. That may seem outdated to you—'

'Very much so. Why should a woman be any more restricted with what she does with her body than a man is?' Zoe slung back at him half beneath her breath.

'I feel guilty that I took that innocence from you,' Raj admitted harshly.

'Even if it's what I wanted? It's not like I'm still a teenager in need of protection,' Zoe argued vehemently, surprised herself to realise how strongly she felt about the decision she had made. 'I just wanted to be like everyone else and know what it was all about instead of feeling…feeling odd,' she framed grudgingly.

'You deserved more than I gave you. It wasn't special…it *should* have been special,' he asserted with conviction.

'Was your first time special for you?' Zoe demanded, cutting in.

Disconcerted by that unexpectedly bold question, Raj gritted his teeth and opted for honesty. 'No.'

'Well, there you are, then, once again you didn't practise what you preach.'

A reluctant laugh was torn from Raj and he

turned to look at her, so tiny she barely reached the centre of his chest and yet in so many ways she was absolutely fearless in her outlook, happy to express her views even when they conflicted with his. She was also too stubborn and independent to even acknowledge his point that if she had valued herself more she would not have entertained surrendering her innocence to him. People rarely confronted Raj with his mistakes or criticised him but Zoe had no such filter. She was quite correct: *he* had dragged *her* into bed.

'And I'm sorry if you don't feel the same way,' she added stiffly, 'but what we shared *did* feel special to me.'

Disconcerted, Raj sent her a gleaming glance and then his lashes dropped low. 'I'm sorry if I upset you but I do hate lies,' he murmured grimly.

'I'm usually very honest but I didn't want you to back off,' Zoe completed unevenly.

'You were curious,' Raj commented, wondering if he had ever had such an extraordinary conversation with a woman before, a conversation in which he was painfully honest and she was as well. He didn't think so and there was something remarkably refreshing about the experience.

'Yes, sorry if that makes you feel a bit like an experiment...but I suppose you were, rather, a new experience, I mean,' she mumbled apologetically.

Exactly like having a day out behind the wheel

of a supercar, Raj thought again with relish, and he burst out laughing. No, no woman had ever dared to tell him before that he was an experiment, but then none had ever used that word, special, for what they had shared with him either. 'Am I allowed to ask how I scored?'

'No. That would be bad for your ego…' Zoe gazed up at him, encountering moonlit dark eyes that shimmered, and her heart skipped a beat.

'You were amazing…and special,' Raj murmured, lifting his hands to gently comb her tousled mane of hair back from her cheekbones, the pads of his fingers brushing the petal-soft skin of her face, sending a quiver of awareness arrowing through her. 'But I shouldn't have touched you. I had no right.'

'We're married.'

'In name only,' he reminded her with scrupulous accuracy, and for some reason she wanted to kick him. 'It's not meant to be real but it's starting to feel very real, which is worrying.'

'Why worrying?' she prompted.

'It wasn't supposed to be like this. We were supposed to live separate lives and make a few public appearances together and that was to be that.'

'So, we departed from the set script. But we're not hurting anyone,' she whispered, her hands settling to his lean waist, her fingers rubbing over smooth, hot skin, feeling the ripple of the muscles of his abdomen pull taut at even that slight touch.

'I don't do relationships,' he reminded her stubbornly even as he leant down to her, drawn by the ripe pink swell of her mouth.

'You're right in the middle of a relationship with me…stop kidding yourself!' Zoe countered. 'Do you think you're about to wake up some morning and find yourself handcuffed to the bed and trapped?'

Raj scooped her slight body up into his arms as if it were the most natural thing in the world to carry her and trudged back up the beach towards the house. 'If it was you cuffing me to the bed, I wouldn't fight and I wouldn't feel trapped,' he muttered huskily.

'That's probably the nicest thing you've ever said to me, but I've got to tell you that cuffing you to the bed looms nowhere on my horizon. If you don't want to be there, you can sleep on the floor,' she told him roundly.

'You said you weren't up for that option.'

'Guess I lied again,' Zoe trilled. 'I could happily consign you to the floor now.'

'And if I *want* to share the bed?' Raj left the question hanging as her lashes opened to their fullest extent, revealing emerald-green enquiry.

'You're welcome,' she said gruffly as he set her

down and she kicked off her flip-flops. 'I think sex makes me hungry… I'm starving again!'

And Raj threw back his head and laughed, stalking over to the concealed fridge, discovering it was packed with prepared food in readiness for such an occasion. Zoe stiffened, marvelling at how relaxed she now felt with Raj. Barriers had come crashing down when they had shared that bed, she acknowledged, but now that she felt closer to him and no longer separate, she was more likely to get hurt. What had happened to her defences? What had happened to her belief that she was only in Maraban to become stronger and more independent? Now she was involved with Raj on a level she had never expected to be and her emotions were all over the place and making her feel insecure.

Zoe froze, frowning as she surveyed the room. 'All the dinner dishes have been cleared away.'

'The staff have been in. Our protection team probably let them know the coast was clear. The bed's probably been changed as well,' Raj forecast.

Zoe gulped. 'It's after midnight, Raj. Don't the staff sleep?'

'They work rotation shifts. Invisible service is a matter of pride to them.'

They ate snacks and she went up to bed first, the exhaustion of the long day crashing down on her all at once. She pillowed her cheek on her hand

and watched Raj strip off his jeans and go for a shower, enviably indifferent to any form of self-consciousness. But then maybe had her body been as flawlessly beautiful as his she would've been equally blasé, she thought sleepily. Instead she was blessed with short legs, tiny boobs and a bottom that was a little big for the rest of her.

'What are we doing tomorrow?' she whispered when he joined her.

'It is already tomorrow,' he pointed out. 'I'm taking you to the old palace where your grandmother grew up and afterwards there'll be an informal meet-and-greet session with the locals and official photographs. My father is making as much possible use of your time in the family as he can.'

'I suppose that was the deal,' she muttered drowsily. 'It'll be interesting seeing where Azra grew up… It was almost as interesting watching your father and my grandfather politely avoid each other at the wedding, and then I was steering clear of your uncle Hakem and he was staying well away from me as well.'

Her brow furrowed at that recollection. Prince Hakem had proved to be a rather colourless little old man and she had been astonished that such a seemingly nondescript personality could be burning underneath with thwarted royal ambitions.

A husky laugh fell from Raj, his breath warming her shoulder. 'My father made a fuss about having your grandfather at the wedding but I talked him round. Stam is, after all, the man who ran off with the Banian princess my father was supposed to marry.'

'But my grandmother, Azra, and your father hadn't even met when she met Stam and fell for him,' Zoe whispered.

'My father still felt it was an insult and it rankled. Go to sleep,' Raj urged. 'This will be another long day but, after the palace visit, we are off the official schedule for the rest of our stay.'

And Zoe thought tiredly of how anxious she had been about having to make any public appearances when she'd first arrived in Maraban and of how inexplicably Raj's presence by her side, or even in the same room, soothed her apprehensions. Somehow, he made her feel safe, protected, as if nothing bad could happen while he was around. It was so silly to endow him with that much importance, she conceded ruefully, and then she slept.

What they had *was* a relationship, Raj recognised with considerable unease. It had become one the minute he married her and intimacy had only deepened the ties and made it more complex. Truly it had been naïve of him not to foresee that development, given the level of attraction they shared Zoe had said it was 'just' sex. Could he believe that, accept that? Was she really sophisticated enough to make that distinction? And could they keep it at that casual level? And in time go their separate ways without regret? It would be like a very long one-night stand, he reasoned while even his brain told him that that was a foolish misconception. He didn't want to treat Zoe the same way he treated his occasional lovers, being distant, keeping it impersonal, always hiding his true self. He felt much more comfortable with Zoe. He wanted to make her happy. For the first time ever with a woman, he would just go with the flow…

Zoe wakened in the morning in Raj's arms. 'Hey, your only body temperature seems to be hot as the fires of hell,' she complained, striving to slide away to cool off.

Raj pulled her back to him with ease and the thrust of his arousal against her stomach made her eyes widen. She looked up at him, all bronzed and in need of a shave, with blue black curls, and he was to die for and there was no denying that she was willing. 'Oh…' she said in entirely another voice.

'If it would be uncomfortable for you…?' he husked, hitching a perfect ebony brow in enquiry.

It probably would be a little bit, she acknowledged, but there was a hungry tingle of awareness heating up between her thighs that made her hips shift with longing. 'No, it wouldn't be,' she lied shamelessly. 'But I need to clean my teeth.'

'No, you don't…you smell like strawberries and woman,' Raj framed thickly, cupping her cheekbones and devouring her mouth as though his life depended on it.

And that was that for Zoe, her heart thumping fit to burst from her chest as her body ratcheted up the scale of arousal as though it had been doing it all her life. When he kissed her, he set her on fire, when he touched her, exploring her urgently sensitive nipples and the tender flesh between her thighs with those long skilful fingers of his, the fire began to blaze out of control and she was turning and twisting, downright writhing with tormented pleasure. By the time he hooked one of her legs over his hips and plunged into her, Zoe was surging towards a climax at an unstoppable pace and the raw, hot excitement of that passionate invasion sent her flying with a choked gasp into the horizon.

'Let's see if you can do that again,' Raj growled as she thrashed under him and he surged into her afresh in a timely change of pace, aiming for long and slow rather than fast and furious.

And she caught her breath again and barely with a quivery little inhale, blonde hair lying in a mad tangle around her head as he rose over and looked down at her, black starlit eyes intent and riveting, her body still singing and pulsing from his last onslaught. His rhythm was sensual, calculated, letting the erotic tension build again and inexorably she shifted from melting to craving. His passion compelled her, and her hands slid over his back, rejoicing in the hard, smooth strength of him as rippling waves began to clench at her pelvis. A wildness took hold of her and she wrapped her legs round him and that final thrust made her soar in an excess of pleasure to the heights again.

Afterwards, he brushed her hair off her damp face and kissed her. 'I hate to hurry you when I've made you late in the first place, but we have to be out of here in an hour if you want to see the palace before we have to face the official welcome…'

'An hour?' she gasped incredulously.

'I'll call your maid and get out of here,' Raj told her helpfully. 'Am I allowed to say that you make a great friend with benefits?'

Was *that* what she was? Zoe thought about that in the shower and pulled a face. It sounded a lot bolder and a lot more laid-back than she believed she was, but who was to say she couldn't change? Wasn't that what her stay in Maraban was aimed at? Finding out who she really was without her sisters and her grandfather wrapping her in cotton wool and watching over her all the time? She was in a brave new world, she reminded herself, and aspects of it were likely to be unfamiliar and scary. Or *sobering*, she conceded ruefully, because her gut instinct was that she didn't want to be a friend with benefits for any man…even Raj.

Her maid had apparently accompanied her from the palace and already had an outfit laid out for her when she reappeared from the bathroom. Zoe cast an eye over the pale green tailored dress and decided it would do very well. At her request her hair was braided, which was cooler in the heat, and when she descended the stairs dead on time, she was smiling, thinking that a maid with hair-styling skills was an invaluable asset and a luxury she had better not become too accustomed to having. It was *all* temporary, she reminded herself, like a winning prize ticket that took her off on an extravagant holiday. Raj was, also, simply a temporary presence in her life. Maybe that was what made the 'friends with benefits' concept meaningless and possibly a little slutty. She winced at that self-judgement.

'You can't wear those shoes trekking round an old building!' Raj exclaimed, engaged in staring at her feet in what appeared to be disbelief.

Zoe sent him a dirty look. 'I'm crazy about shoes, but I'll bring a pair of flats and change into these later,' she conceded reluctantly. 'But don't you get the idea that you have the right to tell me what I should and shouldn't wear… I'm not having that!'

An unholy grin slashed Raj's often serious features as he awaited her reappearance.

The one-time home of the former Banian royal family was huge and sprawling and, although the building had been carefully conserved, it was not used for any purpose other than to house a small museum on the history of Bania and provide the public with the chance to tour Princess Azra's former apartments.

'I wish she hadn't died before I was born.' Zoe sighed, studying old black and white photos of a youthful blonde in local dress. 'Grandad showed me pictures of her. He totally adored her, you know,' she told Raj cheerfully. 'He cast off my father for refusing to do a degree in business and come and work for him. My grandmother told him he was doing the wrong thing and that he should let my dad make his own path but Grandad was too proud and stubborn to listen.'

'It is a challenge for one generation to understand what drives the next. It was years before I could appreciate that in demanding that I marry a woman he chose my father was only asking me to do what he had done himself.'

'But you were in love with someone else,' Zoe reminded him. 'You couldn't possibly have married another woman and made a success of it. You would've been full of bitterness and resentment.'

'My father believes that in our privileged position emotions cannot be allowed to make our decisions for us. I learned the hard way that he was correct,' Raj completed with a harsh edge to his voice.

'You still have to tell me about you and Nabila,' Zoe told him.

'I thought women didn't like a man to talk about previous affairs,' Raj countered in surprise, shooting her a disconcerted glance.

'I'd have to be in love with you to mind that sort of thing and all jealous and possessive and I'm *not*,' Zoe pointed out calmly. 'I'm just being nosy.'

Raj nodded, although the concept shook him because he was unconsciously accustomed to women wanting more from him than he was willing to give, which was why his sensual past consisted of more fleeting encounters than anything else. 'I studied business at one of the Gulf state universities. That's where I met her. Have you ever been in love?' he heard himself ask with astonishing abruptness, but he was, without warning, equally curious.

'No, not even close,' Zoe admitted tightly. 'What happened to me at twelve put me off trying to have a relationship with a man, and then I watched my sisters fall in love and didn't fancy it for myself. There seems to be a lot of angst and drama involved and I'm not into either. So you met Nabila at uni?'

'We were together for two years. I fell hard for her,' Raj bit out grudgingly, while wondering what superhuman qualities it would take to make Zoe fall in love with a man, and then his thoughts became even more tangled because he questioned why he was even thinking along that line. Was it exposure to Zoe? His cousin, Omar, had confided that following his marriage he'd found himself thinking weird thoughts, more like a woman, and that constant female company had that effect on the average man. Raj had to shake his head to clear it and he couldn't grasp how such random ruminations were arising in his usually logical brain.

'Obviously,' Zoe conceded. 'I mean, you weren't likely to defy your father's command for anything less...so you lived together for two years?'

'No, such intimacy was out of the question. If I expected my father to take my wish to marry Nabila seriously, it had to be non-sexual,' Raj proffered curtly. 'He would not have respected anything else.'

Zoe stopped dead and gazed up at him in wonderment. 'Are you saying you didn't sleep with her?'

'Of course, I didn't. My bride had to have an unsullied reputation. It would've been disrespectful to ask my father to countenance any other kind of relationship. He is from a different generation. He does not understand female liberation. In his day a woman's main claim to fame was her purity and a decent woman didn't give it up for anything less than a wedding ring.'

'Gosh, I was cheap,' his bride chipped in, her face suddenly on fire. 'Because as you pointed out, we're not really married in the truest sense of the word.'

'You weren't cheap,' Raj breathed as the museum custodian nervously watched their progress round the exhibits from the other side of the room. Long fingers stroked down her face and lingered below her chin to lift it. 'You were totally incredible and I was unworthy of the gift.'

'That's just flannel,' Zoe informed him, her face warming even more as she connected with brilliant dark eyes that sent butterflies fluttering in her tummy. 'We did what we did because we wanted to.'

'And every time I look at you,' Raj confided thickly, 'I want to do it again.'

'You were telling me about Nabila,' Zoe reminded him doggedly, tiny tingles of arousal coursing through her slight taut length while she fought to suppress those untimely urges. 'Not trying to turn me into a sex maniac.'

'Could I?' Raj asked in a roughened undertone,

those gorgeous eyes pinned to her with a feverish intensity that scorched.

'It's possible,' she downplayed in haste. 'Nabila?'

'She told me she was a virgin because she probably assumed that that was what I wanted to hear. But it wasn't, I wouldn't have cared,' Raj admitted ruefully. 'So naturally I respected what she told me and I was prepared to wait until we were man and wife, but she got bored.'

'Hard to be set on a pedestal and to pretend to be something you're not,' Zoe put in thoughtfully.

'Yes, I did have her on a pedestal.' Raj grimaced. 'I was very idealistic at the age of twenty.'

'You were too young for that size of a commitment,' Zoe commented. 'What happened?'

'I refused to give her up and my father exiled me. It was my final visit and I left Maraban in a hurry. Nabila had given me a key to her apartment and my sudden return was unexpected. That was when I found her in bed with one of her so-called friends. It was clearly a long-standing arrangement and what an idiot I felt!' Raj relived, his superb cheekbones rigid. 'I had surrendered everything for her and there she was, the absolute antithesis of the woman I believed her to be—a shameless cheat and a liar, who only wanted me for my status!'

'And your body, probably,' Zoe told him abstractedly, winning a startled sidewise scrutiny.

'You must've been devastated. I'm lucky. I've never been hurt like that, don't want to be either.'

Raj stared down into her beautiful expressive face and wondered why it was so very easy to talk to her about Nabila, whom he had never discussed with anyone before. It was because she didn't have a personal stake in their marriage, at least not one that he understood, because from what he had observed her new royal status and the awe it inspired meant precious little to her. 'The meet and greet downstairs starts in thirty minutes. You can put on the skyscraper heels if you must.'

'If I *must*?' Zoe queried, slinging him a look of annoyance.

'You struggle to walk in very high heels,' Raj pointed out bluntly.

'Because I never went out anywhere until I came to Maraban. I had this fabulous collection of gorgeous shoes and my sisters borrowed them and I never got to wear them until now,' Zoe told him hotly. 'I'll *learn* to walk in them!'

'Obviously,' Raj countered, realising that he had been tactless in the extreme. 'But why didn't you go out anywhere?'

'I panicked if men came onto me, couldn't handle it,' she confided reluctantly. 'But you don't do that to me for some reason.'

'Maybe because you're not falling for me,' Raj suggested glibly, while cherishing the obvious fact that she felt safer and more protected in his company.

'Yes, that could well be it,' Zoe responded cheerfully as she slid her feet into her high heels while leaning on both his arm and a door handle to balance. 'You wouldn't believe how much more confident I feel standing a few inches taller.'

Watching her sip coffee and smilingly chat by his side only minutes later, Raj decided it had nothing to do with the stupid shoes. He remembered their first meeting and her panic attack and marvelled at how much she had already changed. He had merely met her at a bad moment in a scenario that would have frightened any woman, he recognised. His fingers splayed across her spine and he concealed a grin, thinking about the scratches on his back, badges of pride for a man who knew he had satisfied his woman. Not *his* woman, he immediately corrected himself. Well, she sort of *was* his for the present, an acceptance that somehow lightened the cloud threatening his mood.

It seemed no time at all to Zoe before they were being posed in the palace's grand reception room for the photographs and then they were done, and it was a relief to not be on show any more and know that they had only a holiday ahead of them, she reflected sunnily. They were walking back to the car when a photographer popped out from behind some trees and shouted at them. Half of Raj's security team took off in pursuit of him. At the same time Raj's phone started shrilling and one of the diplomats she had met at the reception emerged with a grim face and moved in their direction with something clutched in his hand.

'What the hell?' Raj groused only half under his breath, pulling out his phone while ensuring that Zoe was safely tucked into the car awaiting them.

She watched as the diplomat proffered the magazine to Raj, saw him glance at it with patent incredulity and then compress his lips so flat they went bloodless. After that he strode back and forth in front of the car talking on his phone, his lean brown hands making angry gestures, his whole stance telegraphing his tense, dissatisfied mood.

'What's happened?' Zoe asked anxiously when he finally came off the phone and climbed in beside her.

CHAPTER EIGHT

'A STORM IN a teacup but it's put my father in a real rage.' Raj expelled a stark breath, impatience and exasperation lacing his intonation. 'Last year my father drove Maraban's only gossip magazine out of the country. Now they're based in Dubai and what they publish about us has steadily become more shocking. He should've left them alone. He has to accept that these days everything we do is watched and reported on and our family cannot hope to keep secrets the way we did when he was a boy.'

'I guess he's a bit behind the times. The press are more disrespectful of institutions nowadays. So, what's in that magazine?' she prompted, thoroughly puzzled. 'Some forgotten scandal?'

'Not even a scandal, merely an intrusion.' He had crushed the magazine between his hands and now he smoothed it out with difficulty and handed it to her. 'Of course, you can't read it but the photos are self-explanatory and this article coming out the same week as our wedding, suggesting that I wasn't allowed to marry the woman I loved because she was a commoner, may be embarrassing for my father but it is also an absurd allegation.'

Dry-mouthed now, Zoe stared down at the splash of photographs, depicting Raj with Nabila. *Old* photos, of course. She could see that they were younger but what she had not been prepared to see was the look of adoration in Raj's face as he gazed down at the other woman. He was studying Nabila as if she'd hung the moon for him and for some reason, Zoe registered, seeing those youthful carefree photos of them holding hands, larking about beside a fountain and smiling at each other *hurt*. She couldn't explain why those photos hurt but the instant she scrutinised them in detail she felt as though someone had punched her hard in the stomach because the pain was almost physical in its intensity.

What the heck was wrong with her? Was she starting to care for Raj? Was she suffering from jealousy, despite her earlier reassurance to him that she felt no such emotion concerning him? Those questions made her feel as shaky as if the ground had suddenly disappeared from under her feet. Yes, she was starting to care in the way you did begin to care more for someone when you got closer to them, she reasoned frantically and, yes, she had been jealous when she saw those photos.

But none of that meant that she was necessarily falling for him.

'She was my first love and that was all,' Raj continued, wonderfully impervious to his bride's pallor and her silence. 'Very few people marry their first love and what does it matter anyway what I was doing *eight* years ago? It's a really stupid article but it *is* revealing a relationship that only our families knew about to the public. What I can't understand is how they got a hold of such private photos. I had copies but I destroyed them after we parted and the friend who took the photos—Omar—would never have shared them with anyone.'

'You said it was an absurd allegation,' Zoe recalled dully. 'How so when it's true? Your father wouldn't agree to you marrying her.'

'Not because of her parentage but because I suspect he had had her checked out and knew a great deal more about her than I knew at the time,' Raj admitted wryly. 'At least he had the consideration not to throw what he had found out in my face.'

'As you said…a storm in a teacup,' Zoe remarked rather stiffly, because all of a sudden she was tired of hearing about anything that related to Nabila and she could only marvel at her previous curiosity. Just then she thought she would be happier if she never heard the wretched woman's name spoken out loud again. As for seeing those stupid photos of her with Raj regarding her as if he had been poleaxed, well, that had been anything but a pleasure for a woman already labelled as a friend with benefits. No doubt that was why she had felt envious of the other woman.

No doubt, right at this very moment Raj was thinking about Nabila, remembering how much he had loved and wanted her, positively *wallowing* in sentimental memories! And on that note, Zoe decided that she would be very, very tired that night, in fact throughout the day, so that Raj would not dare to think she was in the mood to provide any of those benefits he had mentioned!

'You still haven't told me how it happened,' Raj reminded Zoe stubbornly.

Raj was like a dog with a bone when he wanted information, he just kept on landing back on that same avoidance spot of hers, an area of memory where she never ever travelled if she could help it. She breathed in deep, a little bit of a challenge when he was still flattening her to the wall of the shower. Shower sex? Yes, she had gained a lot of experience she had never expected to have over the past two weeks. Resolving to keep her paws off Raj hadn't worked when he was behaving like lover of the year. It was the only analogy she could make when she refused to let herself think of him as a husband.

But there it was: her watch broke, so a new one studded with diamonds arrived within the hour; phone kept on running out of charge, and a new phone was there by bedtime so that she could talk to her sisters as usual. She preferred flowers growing in the ground to those cut off in their prime and stuffed for a short shelf life into vases, and so he took her into the hills of Bania to stage a luxury picnic beside a glorious field of wild flowers. That had been only one of the blinders Raj had played over the past fortnight. He hated her high heels, seemed to be convinced she was going to plunge down steps and, at the very least, break her neck, *but* he had still bought her shoes, the dreamiest, absolutely over-the-top jewel-studded sandals with soaring heels. She had worn them out to dinner last night in a little mountainside inn, where everyone around them had pretended—not very well—not to know who they were to give them their privacy.

The only problem for Zoe, who was blossoming in receipt of such treatment, was that it was a constant battle not to start caring too much about Raj. She kept on reminding herself that none of this was real. Yes, he was her husband, but this was a convenient arrangement that they'd both agreed to. At best, he was just a friend, an intimate friend certainly, but beyond that she knew she dared not go. She was terrified of falling for him and if she made that mistake, she would be rejected and her heart would be broken.

'Zoe...' Raj growled, nipping a teasing trail across the soft skin of her nape to her shoulder with his lips and his teeth, sending a shudder of response through her that even very recent fulfilment could not suppress. 'I want to know how it happened.'

'And I don't want to revisit it.'

'It would be healthier for you to talk about it,' Raj told her doggedly.

'Like you talk about being bullied at military school!' Zoe flung even as she wriggled back into his lean, powerful body, registering that he was ready to go again while conceding that there was nothing new about that because Raj appeared to be insatiable. 'I practically had to cut the story out of you with a knife at your throat,' she reminded him with spirit. 'And by the way, Raj, it wasn't bullying. What you and Omar went through was abuse of the worst kind!'

'If I talked you can talk too,' Raj traded, running a long-fingered hand down over her spine, setting her alight without hesitation.

'This is sexual torture,' she told him shakily.

'All you have to do is say no,' Raj whispered, nipping at the soft lobe of her ear, flipping her long hair over his shoulder as he had learned to do, lost in the magic of her and her response for, as he had learned, it was enthralling to have that much power over a woman, as long as he never ever looked at the other side of the coin and acknowledged the reality that it was mutual.

Zoe straightened her shoulders and breathed, 'Right… I'm saying no…but you're not allowed to look at me like that!'

'Like what?' Raj prompted.

Those stunning dark silvered eyes of his shimmered with hunger and a tiny hint of hurt, and even a hint of hurt on show grabbed Zoe's heart hard and squeezed the breath out of her. She wanted him; every time she looked at him she wanted him.

But that was fine, absolutely fine, she told herself soothingly. It was just sex. She'd had a friend at university who went on a girls' holiday once purely to have sex with a lot of different men. That had been Claire's idea of fun: Raj was Zoe's idea of fun. And the world of sensual freedom she had learned to explore with Raj was the best reward of all. After the shocking attack she had survived as an adolescent, she had never dreamt that she could aspire to such freedom in her own body. Now she could only look back with a sigh when she recalled the frightened, broken young woman she had still been when she'd first met Raj.

'OK… I'll tell you,' she conceded, stepping out of the shower, surrendering to his demand but unable to do so when he was still touching her, something in her shying away in revulsion at any association between making love with Raj and what had happened to traumatise her when she was still a complete innocent.

Zoe settled down on the side of the vast bed, still wet and dripping and not noticing. But Raj noticed, pale beneath his bronzed skin, his sculpted bone structure rigid because he was worried that he had pushed too hard for her confidences. Lifting her up, he carefully wound her like a doll into a giant fleecy towel, but when he tried to keep a soothing hold on her body, she broke away from him and dropped down into a bedside chair instead.

'There was an older boy, well, not much older, he was fourteen and I was twelve,' she trotted out shakily. 'In the same foster home. We used to play video games together… I thought he was a friend. There was a film I wanted to see, a stupid romantic comedy, and my foster mum said he could go with me, look out for me…but he didn't take me to the cinema.'

'You don't have to tell me if you don't want to,' Raj incised in a hoarse undertone.

'No, my sisters used to say I needed to talk about it, which is why I went to therapy. He didn't take me to the cinema. He took me what he said was a shortcut across wasteland and there was this old hut…and I was complaining because there was a storm and I was getting soaked.'

Her breathing was sawing noisily in and out of her struggling lungs.

'In the hut all these boys were waiting. They were a gang and the price of his entry into the gang was to bring a virgin, any virgin. They beat me up when I tried to get away and I was so badly hurt I couldn't move. They cut off my clothes with a kn-knife…and I had nothing even for them to see b-because I was a l-late developer,' she muttered brokenly, almost back there, reliving the terror, the pain and the shame of that public exposure.

Raj grasped both her trembling hands to pull her back into the present. 'It's in the past, and it can't hurt you now unless you let it… And, as you've already told me, you were lucky—you're a survivor.'

'Yes…' Her voice was stronger when she encountered shimmering dark-as-night eyes that seemed full of all the strength and calm she herself so often lacked. 'Yes, you're right. You have to be wondering how I escaped being raped. The police forced their way in to arrest one of the gang and I was rescued. But now you know why I suffer the panic attacks and why I eventually had the nervous breakdown at university—because I hadn't really dealt with what had happened to me. That was when I went for therapy and it helped enormously.'

Raj lifted her fingers to his mouth and kissed

them. His hands were unsteady. All his emotions were swimming dangerously close to the surface and he was fighting to suppress them with every breath in his body. Hers was a distressing story and he now more than understood her fear of men, but there was no need for the rage inside him at those who had been ready to prey on a child for a few moments of vicious entertainment. She had been saved and they had been punished by the law. Only it wasn't enough, he thought fiercely, nowhere nearly enough punishment for the damage that had been inflicted on Zoe. In Maraban, the punishment would have been the death penalty.

As they travelled back to the palace, their honeymoon, as such, at an end, Zoe could see that telling Raj what had happened to her had made him settle back in behind his former reserve. Her small face tightened and her hands gripped together hard. She was questioning why she had shared all her secrets with him and anxious about why she was allowing herself to feel so close to him. Wasn't she acting foolishly? Wasn't it unwise in the circumstances to let every barrier between them drop?

'A surprise awaits you on your return to the palace,' Raj announced, trying to sound upbeat about what he was about to reveal, but failing miserably because he was no idiot and Vivi's cold reaction to him at the wedding had told him all he needed to know about how *he* was viewed by Zoe's family.

'A surprise?' Zoe queried.

He would have to hope that his own surprise went unnoticed while her sister was present. Dark blood highlighted Raj's exotic cheekbones as he thought about the fainting couch he had succumbed to buying and he had to wonder how he had drifted so far from his original intentions. Logic, good judgement and self-control had gone out of the proverbial window the minute he'd laid eyes on Zoe. It was that simple, that *basic*, he acknowledged grimly.

'Raffaele, Vivi's husband, is apparently attending a business meeting in Tasit and your sister accompanied him to visit you.'

To his surprise, Zoe's mouth down-curved and her chin came up, scarcely the display of uninhibited delight he had expected to see in receipt of such news. After all, she was in daily contact with her siblings, revealing a very close bond with them.

Zoe's rarely stirred temper was humming at the prospect of seeing Vivi. Vivi was only coming to visit to check up on her.

'This is a lovely surprise,' Zoe said, smiling and lying through her teeth as she hugged her older sister, wondering when her redheaded sibling would finally accept that she was a grown woman but, by nature, Vivi, a forceful personality, was very protective of those she considered weaker. It stung Zoe's pride to see herself as weak and breakable in Vivi's eyes.

'I wanted to see how you were managing.'

'My phone calls should've reassured you on that score,' Zoe pointed out as a maid brought in coffee and tiny cakes.

Vivi winced. 'Well, to be frank, they had the opposite effect because you sound so gosh-darned happy all the time.'

'My goodness, when did being happy become a sign that there was something to worry about?'

'It's a sign because I've never really heard you this happy before,' Vivi admitted ruefully. 'You can smile and laugh and seem happy on the surface but it's usually very brief and *now*, all of a sudden, when nobody's expecting it...'

'Have you noticed all the changes I've made around here?' Zoe interrupted abruptly, setting down her cup and springing up to indicate all the additional furniture in the room. 'The staff took photos of the unused rooms and sent them while we were away and I made selections. It's a big improvement, don't you think?'

'If medieval makes you hot to trot,' Vivi remarked with a sniff, strolling across the room to flick a heavily carved piece that in her opinion would have looked fabulous in a horror movie of some creepy old house.

'Let me show you around,' Zoe urged, willing to do anything to evade Vivi's curiosity, because in truth she *was* happy and she didn't really want to think too deeply about why.

Vivi glanced into the bedroom, her attention locking straight onto the male and female apparel currently being unpacked by staff. 'So, what happened to the—?'

In haste, Zoe thrust open the bathroom door, although she hadn't yet added anything to its décor, and then froze at the sight of the very opulent tasselled purple fainting couch in the centre.

'Oh, I like *that*…it's sort of sexy and decadent!' Vivi carolled, walking over to smooth a hand across the rich buttoned upholstery and flick a braided gold tassel.

Zoe was recalling her conversation with Raj and her face was burning hot as hellfire even while a little flicker of heat at her core flamed at the gesture…the *challenge*. Would she or wouldn't she? He would be wondering all day about that, she knew he would be, and a dreamy smile at the knowledge of that erotic prospect removed the tension that Vivi's arrival and awkward questions had induced.

'You know, I don't even need to ask you any more.' Vivi sighed as she returned to her coffee.

'Obviously, the separate bedroom deal crashed very quickly and you're sleeping with him. Whose idea was that? I hardly think it was yours! If you get too involved with Raj, Zoe…there will be consequences, because what you have together isn't supposed to last…and where will you be when the marriage ends?'

'It doesn't matter whose idea it was,' Zoe argued quietly. 'All that matters is that there isn't a problem of any kind with Raj and I, and our present arrangements are our private business.'

Vivi groaned out loud. 'You're besotted with him. It's written all over you,' she condemned, her concern palpable. 'That smooth bastard took advantage of you just as I feared he would!'

'Vivi!' Zoe blistered across the room in a furious voice her sister had never heard from her before. 'You do *not* talk about Raj like that!'

'I'm not saying anything I wouldn't say to his face!' Vivi shot back at her defensively. 'I'm trying to protect you but it looks like I got here a little too late for that. Damn Grandad, this is all his fault, his wretched snobbery pushing you into this marriage, and now you're going to get *hurt*.'

Zoe drew herself up to her full unimpressive height. 'There is no reason why I should get hurt.'

'I know what I saw in your face…you're in love with this guy, who only married you to please his father and use our fancy-schmancy grandmother's ancestry to enhance his standing.'

'I'm *not* in love with him,' Zoe argued fiercely. 'It sounds slutty but we're just having sex for the sake of it!'

Vivi unleashed a pained and unimpressed sigh. 'And what would you know about a relationship like that?'

Zoe lifted her head high. 'I'm learning as I go along, just like every other woman has to. I need that freedom, even if I make mistakes… It's part of growing up,' she reasoned.

'You're definitely growing up,' Vivi conceded ruefully. 'I never thought there would come a day when *you* would fight with *me*.'

'Even Winnie fights with you!' Zoe laughed and gave her much taller sister a hug, relieved the unnervingly intimate dispute was over.

After Vivi had been picked up an hour later, Zoe walked thoughtfully back to her suite with Raj. *Not. In. Love. With. Him.* She was simply happy and there was nothing wrong with being happy, was there? Zoe hadn't enjoyed much happiness in her life and she was determined to make the most of every moment.

She studied the fainting couch set out like a statement, an invitation, and she smiled before she wandered down the steps to the private courtyard around which their rooms ranged, which allowed them complete privacy.

And all around her she could see the proof of Raj's desire to please her and make her happy, for the once dark courtyard had been replanted during their absence into a spectacular jungle of greenery amongst which exotic flowers bloomed. Even the fountain she had admired, which had long since fallen out of use, was now working again, clean water sparkling down into the brightly tiled basin below. He hadn't mentioned a word about his intentions, but then he never did. He never looked for thanks either. Gifts simply appeared without fanfare, gifts like the wonderful transformation of an outdated, neglected courtyard garden.

She didn't need him to love her as he had loved Nabila, she only needed the proof that he *cared*, Zoe reflected fiercely. And care he did with amazing efficiency and resolve. How could she expect any more than that in a pretend marriage? After all, he was already giving her much more than she had expected to receive. It wasn't going to last, she knew that, *accepted* that and that was her choice, her choice to live for today and worry about tomorrow only when it arrived…

CHAPTER NINE

ZOE SAT UP in bed and her head swam and her tummy rolled.

Worry gripped her. She had believed she had caught a virus when the symptoms first started but weeks had passed since then and the unwell feeling was lingering, despite the careful diet she had observed. Raj had wanted to get the palace doctor in but she had stalled him once a greater concern began to nag at her nerves.

Zoe grimaced at her pallid reflection in the bathroom mirror. She had lost weight and her eyes looked too big for her face. As soon as the dizziness had evaporated, she went for a shower, striving not to agonise *again* over the reality that she had not had a period since she'd arrived in Maraban. After all, she couldn't possibly be pregnant even if the light head, the nausea and her tender breasts reminded her of what her sisters had experienced during pregnancy. How could she be pregnant when Raj had not once run the risk of getting her pregnant? But, she did recall once, weeks ago in the shower when he had overlooked the necessity and she had meant to mention it but hadn't been worried enough to do so.Now she wished she had pointed out that oversight.

Of course no method of birth control was infallible, another little voice nagged at the back of her head. And how on earth was she to put her worries to rest when the acquisition of a pregnancy test in secret had so far proved beyond her capabilities. She never got the opportunity to leave the palace alone. She was surrounded by security and all too many helpful people when she went out. Let's face it, Zoe, she thought forlornly, the Crown Princess of Maraban cannot be seen buying a pregnancy test without causing a furore. It was ironic that what would have thrilled the population filled Zoe with sick apprehension because she couldn't forget Raj saying that such a development would be a disaster in their situation.

Of course, it would be when it was only a pretend marriage and if she had a boy, he would be next in line to the throne. If she was pregnant and it was a boy, she would have to live in Maraban for at least the next twenty years as Raj's ex-wife and she certainly didn't fancy that option as a future. She would have to sit on the outskirts of his life, watching him marry another woman and have a family with her. Naturally, Raj would move on after their marriage ended but she certainly didn't want to sit around nearby to actually *watch* him doing it.

When she emerged from her bedroom, dressed in a pastel-blue dress with her hair in a braid and her make-up immaculate, Bahar, her PA—or social secretary, as Zoe preferred to think of the young attractive brunette—awaited her with a list of her appointments. It pleased her tremendously that after three months away from home she had now acquired the confidence to handle visiting schools and such places without having to drag Raj everywhere with her for support. Coming to Maraban and marrying Raj had been the best decision she had ever made when it came to getting stronger and moving forward with her life.

As her breakfast was brought to the table, Zoe's stomach lurched even as she looked at it and she pushed the plate away and settled for a cup of tea. After all, she couldn't afford to eat if she was going out to an official engagement where her succumbing to a bout of sickness in public would be a serious embarrassment, she reflected with an inner shudder at the prospect. She would catch a snack later, by which time hopefully the nausea would have subsided.

Walking down the last flight of stairs, she was wondering whether or not to call in on Raj in his office when she broke out in a cold sweat. Her legs wobbled under her and she snatched at the stone balustrade to stay upright but the sick dizziness engulfing her was unstoppable and as she lurched to one side, dimly conscious that someone was seizing hold of her from behind, she passed out.

When Zoe came around slowly, she winced at the sensation of a needle in her arm and gripped the hand that was holding hers in dismay. Her eyes fluttered open as Raj leant down to her saying, 'Don't try to get up in case you faint again. Dr Fadel decided a blood test would be a good idea… sorry about that.'

The very quietness of his voice made her scan the room behind him, which seemed to be filled to the brim with anxious-looking people. Mortification made her close her eyes again and do as she was told because she had a clear recollection of almost tumbling down that last flight of stairs.

'I'll be late for my appointment,' she protested.

'You will not be leaving the palace today.'

'But...'

'Not until the doctor has diagnosed what is wrong with you,' Raj spelt out more harshly, in a tone she wasn't accustomed to hearing from him.

In shock at that attitude, she glanced up at him, but he had already moved away to speak to the older man closing a doctor's bag on the desk. She registered that she was in Raj's office on the sofa he had slept on when they were first married, and very slowly and carefully she began to inch up into a sitting position.

Raj stalked back to her. 'Stay flat and lie still,' he told her wrathfully.

He was furious with her, Zoe realised in consternation, wondering why. Possibly the uproar her faint had caused, she reflected unhappily, because the room was still crammed with staff all trying to speak to Raj at once in his own language, so she could only follow one word in three that she was hearing and those were the simple ones. Her ambition to learn Arabic was advancing only slowly. Finally, the room cleared and they were alone again.

'May I sit up now or are you going to get angry again?' Zoe murmured.

Raj gazed across the office at her and then moved forward before hovering several feet from her as though an invisible wall had suddenly come down between them. 'I apologise. I was not angry with you, I was angry with myself for neglecting your health,' he admitted tautly. 'I knew you were unwell but I listened to you when you refused to let me call the doctor in. I *shouldn't* have listened!'

'Raj, that was *my* fault, this stupid virus, and I'm not awfully fond of medics.'

'You will want to express thanks to your bodyguard, Carim. He saved your life when he prevented you from falling down the stairs. At the very least you would have been badly hurt with broken limbs,' Raj framed jaggedly, his hands clenching into fists by his side. 'But such a fall could definitely also have killed you and nothing is worth that risk.'

'Of course, it isn't,' Zoe agreed soothingly because she was shaken as well by the accident that she had so narrowly escaped. 'OK, you were right and I was wrong.'

'I swore to look after you and I have failed in my duty,' Raj informed her hoarsely.

Zoe paled. 'It's not your duty, Raj. I'm a fully grown adult and I made an unwise decision when I chose not to consult a doctor. Please don't blame yourself for my mistake.'

'How can I do anything else?' Raj shot back to her with seeming incredulity. 'You are my wife and you are in a country foreign to you. Who else should stand responsible for your well-being?'

I'm not your *real* wife. The declaration sprang to her lips but she didn't voice it, belatedly recognising that whether Raj viewed her as his real wife or otherwise he would still feel that it was his duty to ensure her well-being. Three months ago she would happily have flung that declaration of independence at him but now she knew him a little better, knew the crushing weight of responsibility he took on without complaint. As his father, the King, suffered increasing ill health and days he was unable to leave his quarters, more of his obligations were falling on Raj's shoulders. Unsurprisingly, Raj didn't have an irresponsible bone in his lean, beautiful body and he was infuriatingly good at blaming himself for any mishap or oversight.

'I'm sorry if I seemed to speak rudely and angrily,' Raj breathed tautly, silvered dark eyes locked to her lovely face. 'But I was very concerned.'

'I understand that and I'm fine. In fact I think I'm recovered enough now to make that appointment.'

'No, they will have to settle for me doing it in your place,' Raj sliced in forcefully. 'You're not going out anywhere until we have heard from the doctor—'

'Raj, for goodness' sake, I'm fine,' she told him again, swinging her feet down onto the floor to punctuate the statement.

'We'll see,' Raj asserted with tact as he reached for her hand to help her upright, tugging her close to him, his stunning dark deep-set eyes below his straight black brows roaming over her delicate face. 'But we will not see today...however, I am free this evening, and if you were to feel strong enough to welcome me home on that couch, I would be extraordinarily pleased.'

Zoe gurgled with laughter and stretched up on tiptoe to taste his wide sensual mouth with her own. And that was that, he was magically distracted from his overwhelming anxiety about her welfare. Her heart hammered and her fingers closed into his shirtfront because she wanted to rip it off him. Against her, she could feel him hard and ready and hunger coursed through her, turning her wanton with need.

With an enormous effort, Raj set her back from him. 'We *can't*. People are waiting for my arrival,' he reminded her raggedly. 'But it is one of those occasions when I wish I had the freedom to tell everyone but you to go to hell!'

Zoe flushed, censuring herself for tempting him merely to distract him because it had been a selfish move and he was never selfish, which made her feel bad. On the other hand, the couch invitation was welcome, she acknowledged with a tiny shiver of anticipation, wondering what had happened to the genuinely shy young woman she had been mere months earlier. She wasn't shy with Raj. In fact, she was doing stuff with Raj she had never dreamt she would ever do with any man, once alien things like purchasing very fancy lingerie and posing in it, revelling in the rush of powerful femininity his fierce desire for her and his equally audacious appreciation gave her every time. She had discovered a whole new self to explore and secretly it thrilled her.

Outside the office door, she thanked the guard who had saved her from falling and he grinned at her, telling her in broken English that he would have died sooner than let anything happen to her on his watch. His undeniable sincerity shook her and she climbed the stairs, thinking that until now she hadn't quite grasped how the people around her and those she met during engagements viewed her as Raj's wife, certainly hadn't taken that level of care and concern as seriously as they did. It struck her that many of those same people would be disappointed when she and Raj split up. But then there was nothing she could do about that, was there? She was a sham wife but *they* didn't know that, didn't know that she was nothing more than a glossy convenient lie foisted on the public, she ruminated unhappily.

She was having lunch when the middle-aged doctor she had glimpsed in Raj's office called to see her. Dr Fadel was King Tahir's doctor and resident in the palace and, fortunately for her, he had qualified in London and spoke excellent English.

After the usual polite pleasantries, he asked if he could dismiss the hovering staff and she nodded acquiescence with a slight frown, her tension rising. Of course, he was about to tell her that her hormones were all out of kilter, which was the most likely diagnosis, and she didn't want to discuss her absent menstrual cycle with an audience either.

'I am blessed to be the doctor to break such

momentous news,' he then informed her with a beaming smile. 'You have conceived, Your Royal Highness…'

'Conceived...?' Zoe repeated as if she had never heard the word before, and she tottered back down into the seat she had vacated to greet him, so great was the shock of that announcement. That her deepest fear had been confirmed rocked her world to its foundations.

'The blood test was positive. Of course, it is impossible for me to tell you anything more without a further examination.' He looked at her enquiringly. 'Would that be in order? Or would you prefer another doctor, perhaps a specialist, to give you further information? I'm not inexperienced. I do have many female patients in the royal household.'

Zoe was in a daze. She pushed her hands down on the table to rise again. *Pregnant?* she was screaming inside her head, still wondering if it could be a mistake and willing to subject herself to any check-up that could possibly reveal his diagnosis *was* a mistake, she reasoned fearfully as she followed him from the room and he lamented the lack of lifts in the palace. A lift would have to be installed immediately, the doctor began telling her, particularly when her near accident earlier was taken into consideration. A pregnant woman couldn't be expected to run up and down flights and flights of stairs, particularly not a woman carrying a child he described as 'so precious a child for Maraban'.

It wouldn't be precious to Raj, Zoe thought miserably, not to a man who had frankly referred to such an unlikely event as a *disaster*. Suddenly she was in total conflict with herself and split into two opposing halves. On the one hand she adored children and she very much wanted her baby if she did prove to be pregnant, but on the other, she was sort of guiltily hoping that the doctor's verdict was wrong because of the way Raj would feel about it and that felt even more wrong.

A glimpse of the trim and determined little nurse who had jabbed her with a syringe the night she was kidnapped was not a vote winner in the troubled mood she was in, but Zoe refused to react, deeming her potential pregnancy more important as she lay down on an examination couch and an ultrasound machine was wheeled in. An instant later she heard the whirring sound of her baby's fast heartbeat and she paled, feeling foolish for thinking that the doctor could have been in error. It was an even greater surprise to discover that she was already three months along and almost into the second trimester, which meant that she had conceived very early in their marriage.

The doctor happily dispensed vitamin tablets and congratulated her on her fertility, studying her literally as if she were a walking miracle. She supposed in comparison to the last generation of the royal family, she did strike him that way because it had taken over thirty years and three wives to produce Raj.

'The King will be overjoyed,' he told her cheerfully.

'Oh, but...' Zoe hesitated, questioning if it was even possible to keep a lid on such a revelation within the palace.

'The King needs this good news, with his health as precarious as it has been,' his doctor assured her with gravity.

'Then my husband can tell him after I have *first* told *him*,' Zoe countered firmly.

But on one level she thought she was probably wasting her breath because the cat was out of the bag and there was nothing she could do about that: the doctor, the nurse and whoever had done the blood test already knew of her condition. Just how fast the news had spread was borne out only minutes later when she returned to her room and was ushered into the bedroom where tea, a ginger biscuit and the book she had been reading awaited her by the bed like a heartfelt invitation to rest as pregnant women were so often advised to do. Smothering a groan, she lay down, ironically worn out by the day she had had. Off came her shoes and then her dress and she lay back, confronted by the daunting evening lying ahead of her because she had no choice other than to tell Raj immediately. Would it sound better if she did the couch thing first? Or would that look manipulative?

In the event, she didn't get to make that decision because she slept through most of the afternoon, only wakening when the sound of a door closing jolted her awake. She opened her eyes on Raj striding towards the bed and the slumberous expression in his shimmering dark scrutiny as he looked at her lying there in her flimsy underwear. He sank down on the edge of the bed. 'How are you feeling now?'

'OK—hungry now that the sickness has taken a break. Dr Fadel said that with a little luck that should start fading soon,' she told him tightly. 'You see, I'm *not* ill as such. I'm pregnant…'

As she hesitated, her nerves getting the better of her for a moment, she studied Raj; his lean, darkly handsome features had locked tight, his jaw line clenching hard.

'I think it must've been that time in the shower just after the wedding. You forgot to use anything. I should've said something then but I really didn't think anything would come of it,' she acknowledged uncomfortably, wishing he would say something.

Raj blinked because for an instant his surroundings had vanished; what she had told him had to be the very last development he had expected, but it also led to a revelation that hit him even harder. He turned pale, in the matter of a moment recognising the situation he was in.

'We've barely got out of bed to eat for three months,' Raj breathed in a rueful undertone. 'What can I say? I was in charge of contraception and I forgot. So, we are going to become parents...forgive me, I am stunned by the concept of something so surprising.'

'You said it would be a disaster if I became pregnant,' Zoe reminded him uncertainly, still unable to read his mood, particularly when he sprang upright again and started pacing across the floor, clearly too restless to stay seated.

'A disaster more from your point of view than from mine,' Raj qualified with level clarity. 'We agreed to part but I cannot agree to let you leave me carrying our child and I do not want our child raised without either one of us. Surely we are doing well enough together for you to stay in our marriage for some time to come?' A straight ebony brow lifted enquiringly, intense dark eyes scanning her triangular face for an answer. 'Could you accept that? If we remain married, we can raise our child together.'

A quivery little breath ran up through Zoe, allowing her lungs to function again. The backs of her eyes prickled and stung. Until Raj had asked her to *stay* married to him, she had not realised how horribly tense she had become and the painful tension slowly ebbed out of her stiff muscles.

'So, we just go on as normal?' Zoe checked.

'Why not? Are we not both content as we are?' Raj prompted tautly.

Zoe nodded but couldn't help wishing he could be a little more emotional about staying married to her. There she went again, wanting what she couldn't have, she scolded herself, because she knew herself better now. She could look back and recognise the raging jealousy that had assailed her after seeing those photos of Raj with Nabila that had so clearly depicted his love for the beautiful brunette. There was nothing she could do about such feelings except keep them under control and hidden. And considering the circumstances in which they had married, each for their own very practical reasons, it was illogical and pathetic to long for Raj to fall in love with her as well.

'You said…"stay in our marriage for *some time to come*",' Zoe recited tightly. 'What sort of time frame were you considering?'

At that question for further clarification, Raj stiffened and raked long brown fingers through his tousled black curls. 'Must we be so precise?'

Zoe swallowed hard at the edge of reproof in his tone. 'Well, it would be easier for me to know how *you* see the future.'

'With you and our child together. I would impose no limits. I would like to throw away *all* the boundaries we agreed and make this a normal marriage,' Raj spelt out without hesitation. 'I still can't believe that you're pregnant.'

'Neither can I,' Zoe revealed, scrambling off the bed only to be immediately caught up into his strong arms.

'I didn't think it could happen that easily…it is a brilliant accident,' Raj murmured with husky conviction as he came down on the bed with her. 'Are we still allowed to share this bed?'

'Of course, we are. I've been fully checked out.' A kind of sick relief combined with dizzy happiness was filtering through Zoe as she dimly acknowledged that he was giving her what she most wanted. She wasn't going to have to give him up like the salted caramel ice cream she had recently become addicted to, she was going to get to *keep* him. Of course, it wasn't perfect, she conceded reluctantly, not when he only wanted her to stay married to him because she was pregnant. Even so, being accepted as a normal wife was a huge upgrade on being labelled a friend with benefits.

'What are you thinking about?' Raj chided, lying back on the bed with his gorgeous dark eyes fiercely welded to her reflective face.

'Nothing remotely important,' she told him, and she meant it when she said it even if she dimly understood even then that sooner or later she would once again fall into the trap of craving more than he had to give her.

He toyed with her mouth, soft and gentle, and then nipped wickedly at her bottom lip with the edge of his teeth. Her hands lifted and her fingers speared into his black curls, liquid heat pooling in her pelvis as he deliberately snaked his lean hips into the junction of her thighs, the thrust of his arousal unmistakeable. He was always so hot for her. It was enough, it was more than enough to be desired, cared for, appreciated. Even if she felt as though she was keeping him by default? She crushed the thought, burying it deep. She already had more with him than she had ever thought she would have, so craving anything else would be greedy.

'I want you so much,' Raj confided rawly, sitting up over her to wrench off his shirt, yank roughly at his tie. 'Knowing my baby is inside you is so sexy…'

Zoe blinked. It *was*? He was lifting her to deftly undo her bra, groaning with satisfaction when her small pouting breasts came free to hungrily claim an engorged nipple with his mouth. A gasp was wrenched from her as he teased the other with his fingers. 'You're more sensitive there than ever,' he husked. 'I love your body.'

She knew he did: he never left it alone. He couldn't walk past her without touching her in some way and if they were alone, it almost always concluded in their bed, although they had succumbed to christening his office sofa a time or two and they had once had sex in a limousine on a long drive. He had an astonishingly strong sexual appetite. Anyone watching him could have been forgiven for thinking he hadn't had the freedom to enjoy her for a couple of days at least but that was not the case.

He tugged off her panties and yanked down the zip in his trousers, shedding his clothing with an impatience that never failed to add to her excitement. There he was, all sleek and golden and beautiful, and he was finally hers to keep like a precious possession she had been fighting for without even appreciating what she was doing or even what was happening inside her own head. She had wanted love but then what woman didn't? If *he* could settle for less, she could settle, she reasoned as he snaked down her body with darting little kisses and caresses that set her on fire, ultimately settling between her spread thighs to pleasure her in the way he enjoyed the most.

As a rippling spasm of pleasure gathered low in her body, she clutched at his hair, writhed, squirmed, begged until at last she climaxed in an explosive surge that certainly didn't feel in any way as though she were settling for less. Raj shifted over her then, hungrily kissing her, and the excitement began to rocket again as he sank into her with delicious force, pushing her legs back to deepen his penetration. Definitely not less, she told herself as she rose breathlessly to meet his every thrust, every move instinctive and raw with the excitement she could barely contain. There was more and then even more of that insanely thrilling pleasure before he sent her flying into a wild breathless climax that shattered her senses and her control, leaving her slumped in a wreck of heavy, satiated limbs in the aftermath.

She hadn't heard a phone ring, had been too far gone, but she surfaced when she realised that Raj wasn't holding her close as he usually did. She turned over, saw him talking urgently on his phone while he strode about, naked and bronzed and muscular, and she propped her chin on the heel of her hand, enjoying watching him. That enjoyment gradually faded when he went on to make several other quick calls in succession, alerting her to the knowledge that something must have happened, and because his expression changed from smiling to grim she couldn't tell whether what had happened was a good or bad thing.

'I'm afraid I'm going to have to leave you for the night,' Raj told her with a frown. 'The construction workers have stumbled on archaeological remains at the Josias site.'

'The hospital project in the capital of Maraban?'

'It's potentially a very exciting discovery but

it means that the site has to close until we can get an official inspection done tomorrow, and that throws the whole project and the work crews into limbo. I'm flying out there now to meet with the managers and look at contingency plans. It is possible that we won't be able to build there at all,' he concluded gravely. 'And the hospital is very much needed in that area.'

Recalling that Nabila was the CEO of the construction firm involved, Zoe sat up, her pale hair falling round her flushed face, because she knew he was undoubtedly about to meet the other woman again for the first time in eight years and she very much wanted to be in the vicinity. 'I could come with you!' she said in sudden interruption.

'No, not this time. What would be the point? I'm likely to be in meetings most of the night and certainly all of tomorrow, sorting this out,' he told her dismissively as he strode into the bathroom.

'I would still like to have gone,' Zoe confided in a small voice to an empty room.

But did she really need to cling to him like glue? she reproved herself. There were few things more distasteful to a man than a clingy, needy and jealous woman and Raj would quickly get tired of her if she started acting paranoid and suspicious purely because he was mixing with his ex-girlfriend in a business environment. She had to grow up, she told herself urgently, not react to her stabbing insecurity with adolescent immaturity. After all, nothing was likely to change in the short term. She was pregnant and *really* married now.

And how did Raj truly feel about that development? It shocked Zoe to accept that she had not the smallest idea of how *he* felt, and the instant she registered that worrying truth, another little brick of security tumbled down from her inner wall of defences. Sadly, there was no ignoring the truth that the closest Raj had actually come to expressing his personal feelings was the assurance that he regarded her being pregnant with his child as…sexy. Although he had labelled her conception a brilliant accident, which did suggest he was pleased.

Zoe grimaced. Why couldn't he simply have said so, openly? In reality, now that she was recalling that conversation, she realised that Raj had not expressed a single emotion, which for an emotionally intense man of his ilk was not reassuring, she reflected worriedly.

Were duty and a sense of responsibility for his child all that had driven Raj's request that she stay married to him?

And if that *was* the case, what could she possibly do about it?

CHAPTER TEN

RAJ'S PHONE RANG constantly right up until he left the palace. He was feeling guilty because Zoe had been very quiet when he left. But there was no way he would have considered dragging her across country late at night, especially now that she was pregnant and he had no idea where he would be staying. Zoe looked frail for all her lack of complaint. She had lost her appetite, dropped in weight. Yet even though he had noticed he had said and done nothing because it had not even occurred to him that she could be pregnant. What kind of husband was he? Not a very good one, he decided grimly.

And now he was to become a father. A dazzling smile flashed across his lean dark features. That was a marvellous development, a near miracle in their circumstances.

His phone rang again as he awaited his limo in the forecourt of the palace and he dug it out, only to freeze in surprise as the caller identified himself for, although he had met the man, his royal status ensured that he wasn't especially friendly with anyone in that profession, and the warning the journalist gave Raj astonished him. He immediately called Omar and passed it on to him and Omar announced that he would be travelling to the hospital site as well.

In the early hours of the following morning, having dealt with a torch-lit visit to the site and with wildly excited archaeologists, who were hopeful that the legendary lost city built by Alexander the Great had been discovered on Marabanian soil, Raj was more than ready for his bed. He walked into the comparatively small hotel closest to the site. He was relieved that he hadn't succumbed to the temptation of bringing Zoe because he did not think the level of comfort on offer sufficient for a pregnant woman. As his father had remarked in wonderment when he had phoned him earlier to break their news, Zoe would have to be treated from now on like the Queen she would one day be.

Raj was smiling at the memory and sharing it with his cousin, Omar, who was beside him as he pushed open the door of his room. And then quite forcibly the warning he had received, and begun to discount because he had yet to even *see* Nabila, was revived because Nabila sat up in the bed that should've been his, the sheet tumbling to reveal her bare breasts. Filled with angry distaste at her brazen display, Raj averted his eyes, unimpressed by the expression of seemingly embarrassed innocence she had put on when she glimpsed Omar by his side.

'For goodness' sake, tell Omar to *leave*,' Nabila urged Raj.

'I'm staying,' Omar delivered with satisfaction, never having liked the brunette even when Raj had been in love with her. 'But it is gratifying to discover that you can sink even lower than I expected.'

Raj strode to the foot of the bed. 'What the hell are you playing at?' he demanded.

Deciding to ignore Omar, Nabila focused her eyes on Raj with blatant hunger. 'I want you and I really don't care what I have to do to get you this time around. Isn't that enough?' She treated him to a look of languorous enticement. 'Don't tell me you're not still curious about what it would be like between us.'

Raj's mouth curled with disgust and he swung round to stalk back to the door and address his protection team in the corridor. 'Get her out of here… and find me another room,' he ordered impatiently.

'I'm not asking for marriage this time around,' Nabila crooned behind him. 'I would be your mistress…your every secret fantasy.'

'My *wife* is my every secret fantasy,' Raj countered drily as he strode out.

* * *

At dawn, Raj was enjoying a working breakfast on the terrace at his hotel with Omar and the management team of Major Holdings, including the CEO, Nabila, who had contrived to take a seat opposite him. He ignored her to the best of his ability, barely even turning his head when she spoke.

'Raj!' she exclaimed, startling him while simultaneously reaching for his hand.

For a split second, he was so disconcerted by that unanticipated over-familiarity and the pleading expression she wore on her face that he did nothing and then he freed his fingers with a sudden jerk and leant back in his chair, cursing himself for not having reacted more immediately to the threat. For Nabila *was* a threat, he acknowledged in a sudden black fury, a threat to his marriage. At that moment, he had not the slightest doubt that a photographer was hiding somewhere in the vicinity, most probably one with a telephoto lens, and had captured that image of them holding hands and that that stolen photo was intended for publication with the presence of their companions eradicated.

A couple of hours later, because she was sleeping in, Zoe turned over in bed, drowsily wondering what had wakened her and failing to notice that her mobile phone was flashing on the cabinet to one side of her. She stole her hand across to the other side of the bed and then remembered that Raj was gone for the night. With a dissatisfied sigh, she dragged her fingers back from that emptiness and reminded herself that it was mortifyingly clingy to want him there *every* night. She could be perfectly happy without him, of course she could be! With no suspicion of just how soon that assumption was to be tested, Zoe went back to sleep.

Zoe wakened in astonishment to find her sisters beside her bed and blinked in disbelief. 'What are you two doing here at this hour of the day?' she demanded.

'We were shopping in Dubai so we didn't have far to come,' Winnie explained stiffly. 'We want you to come home with us. Grandad agrees.'

Zoe sat up. 'Why on earth would you want me to come home with you?'

'*Because*,' Vivi said bluntly, 'Raj is playing away behind your back and you're in love with the rat!'

Zoe frowned. 'No. Raj wouldn't do that to me,' she said with perfect assurance because, in that line, she trusted him absolutely.

Winnie shoved a mobile phone in front of her gaze. Her lashes fluttered in bewilderment and then she focused and saw Raj with the *one* woman in the world she wouldn't trust him with. Raj in a photo holding hands with Nabila, his lean, darkly handsome features very serious, her face beseeching. Beseeching *what* from him? Zoe broke out in a sudden sweat and then just as quickly, as familiar queasiness assailed her, was forced to leap out of bed and push past her sisters to make it to the bathroom in time to be sick.

'Where did you see that photo? Raj only left last night,' she reasoned when she was able to respond, wondering exactly *when* that photo had been taken and then questioning whether the timing even mattered.

'That photo was offered to Grandad for sale first thing this morning,' Winnie told her in disgust. 'I imagine it was taken by some greedy paparazzo, who worked out what that picture would be worth on the open market.'

As Zoe drooped over the vanity unit brushing her teeth, still weak with nausea and dizziness, Vivi tugged her gently away and settled her down on the fainting couch. 'Take a deep breath and keep your head down. What's the matter with you? Are you ill?'

'Pregnant,' Zoe whispered, still in shock at that photo, fighting to withstand the great tide of pain threatening to engulf her. Raj had refused to take her with him the night before...*no wonder*! Had he known even then that he wanted the freedom to be with his ex-girlfriend?

'Pregnant?' Vivi gasped and her sisters engaged in a lively argument above her head, which Zoe was content to ignore because infinitely more im-

portant decisions loomed ahead of her, she grasped dully.

How could she remain married to a man in love with another woman and already seeing her behind her back? Holding hands with her? Although that was the least that had probably gone on between them, she recognised sickly, for it was unlikely that Raj and Nabila would not finally have taken the opportunity to have sex. Particularly not when, in that photo, they were staring at each other like long-lost lovers reunited.

'I'll be frank,' Vivi murmured with surprising quietness. 'You're in love with Raj and he's hurting you and we love you enough that we can't just stand back and allow that.'

'I'm *not* in love with him,' Zoe lied, her eyes watering in a last-ditch effort to save face with her sisters.

But there it was: the truth she had suppressed and refused to face except in the secret depths of her heart. She had fallen madly in love with her fake husband and for all the wrong reasons. Reasons like his smile and the sound of his voice and the raw power of his body over hers in bed. Reasons like the English breakfast tea he had ordered on her behalf and the glorious shoes he'd bought her and had put in the dressing room without even mentioning the purchases. Reasons that encompassed a hundred and one different things and many that she would have found hard to put into words.

Winnie's eyes were also brimming with tears. 'Come back with us to Athens...*please*!'

And Zoe's first reaction was to say no, until she considered the alternatives. She could confront Raj and he would probably admit the truth, which would not be a comfort to her. She could pretend she hadn't seen the photograph and silently agonise over it and that prospect had even less appeal. Or she could take advantage of a breathing space in which to decide what she would do next, she reasoned bravely. It wouldn't be running away, she ruminated, it would be giving herself the time to control her emotional reaction and behave like an adult and deal with the situation. If she stayed, she might cry and let him see that she had been hurt, and what was the point of that?

But what if Raj had not actually cheated on her? Raj was not by nature a cheat, she reasoned, wondering if she was clutching at straws when she thought along such lines. Naturally she didn't want to think he could've been unfaithful, but Nabila was different, Nabila was in a class of her own because once Raj had *loved* her. Could he have resisted the chance to finally be with the woman he had once loved? And wasn't hoping he might have resisted only proof that Zoe was weakly willing to make excuses for him? Shame drenched her pale cheeks with hot pink and she decided to listen to her sisters, who had much more experience than she did with men. If Winnie and Vivi both believed that Raj had succumbed to Nabila's wiles, they were probably right. She trusted their judgement more than she trusted her own because she was all too well aware that her feelings for Raj coloured her every conviction and that she wasn't capable of standing back and making an independent call.

Zoe had her maid pack only one suitcase, because there was no advantage in advertising the fact that she was leaving and would probably never return to the royal palace. She would send for the rest of her stuff later but when she thought about that, thought about the wardrobe Raj had bought her, thought about his favourite outfits, she as quickly decided that she wanted nothing that would only serve to keep unfortunate memories alive.

Her protection team accompanied her to the airport and flatly refused to leave her there. Suppressing a sigh, she let them board her grandfather's private jet with her, knowing that Raj would recall them later after he had read her note and had seen the photo she had sent to his phone. He wouldn't require any other explanation for her departure because he was definitely not stupid.

When that photo came up on his phone, forwarded by Zoe, Raj succumbed to a rage that almost burned him alive and it took Omar stepping in to prevent him from telling Nabila in front of an audience what he thought of her filthy tactics. Omar's intervention ensured that he did what he had to do at the site, which was his duty, and went home as soon as he possibly could to talk to his wife. A single-line note informing him that she would never 'share' a man greeted his return.

The discovery that she had been removed by her siblings and flown to her grandfather's home in Greece came as a complete shock. It was closely followed by a terse phone call from Stamboulas Fotakis, who accused him of disrespecting his grandchild in a grossly offensive public disregard of his marital status. And as if those punishments were not sufficient, he was summoned by his father, who in his ineffable highly efficient way knew exactly what was happening in his son's marriage and pointed out that his son only had himself to thank for allowing a harpy like Nabila within a hundred yards of him.

'When you bring your wife home again, I will have Nabila thrown out of the country,' the King pronounced with satisfaction.

'Let us hope I can bring Zoe home,' Raj breathed with difficulty, mastering his temper but only just in the face of that provocation, for throwing Nabila out of Maraban would only create a scandal that Nabila would relish.

His arrival in Greece late that night was punctuated by further unwelcome attacks. Zoe was in bed and not to be disturbed, according to Stam Fotakis. 'She's fragile,' he told Raj in condemnation. 'She needs protection from those who would use her soft heart against her.'

'I would not use…'

Her sister, Vivi, walked into her grandfather's office and proceeded to try and tear strips off Raj but Raj wasn't taking that from anyone, least of all Zoe's fiery sibling, and an almighty row broke out before Stam ran out of patience and demanded that both of them go to bed. 'If you must, you may speak to Zoe in the morning,' he informed Raj in a ringing tone of finality.

But Raj wasn't about to be steered in a direction he didn't want to go. He let himself be shown to a guest room without any intention of *waiting* until he could see *his* wife. As soon as he was alone, he learned where her room was by the simple measure of contacting her protection team.

Zoe was curled up on a lounger on the balcony beyond her room, watching the sea silver and darken in the moonlight. Misery felt like a shroud tightly wrapped round her, denying her the air she needed to breathe. She had still to accept the concept of a life empty of Raj. Every time she contemplated that terrifying prospect, she felt as though someone were flaying the skin from her bones, only the pain was internalised. How had one man become so important to her survival that her entire world had begun to revolve around him? It both shocked and incensed her that she could have been weak and foolish enough to fall in love with a man she had known from the outset would never be hers on any permanent basis.

When the patio doors behind her slid open, she flinched, expecting it to be one of her sisters, come yet again to offer depressing advice. She didn't want the assurance that she would get over Raj. She didn't want to be told that there would eventually be another man worthier of her love in her future when just then, and against all reason and logic, all her body and her brain cried out for *was* Raj.

'Zoe…?'

In astonished recognition of that dark deep accented intonation, Zoe was startled and she leapt off the lounger and spun round. *'Raj?'* she gasped incredulously.

'Hush…' Raj put a finger to his lips in warning. 'I wouldn't put it past your family to try and drag me out physically and I don't want a fight breaking out between my protection team and your grandfather's. But I will allow no man on earth to tell me *when* I can see my wife.'

'But I'm not your wife—not really your wife,' Zoe protested. 'And I *never* was.'

Raj studied the pale triangle of her face in the moonlight and guilt cut through him because it was *his* fault that she had been hurt and upset. 'I have to explain what happened with Nabila.'

'No, you don't owe me any explanations!' Zoe cut in hastily. 'But you can't expect me to live with you and turn a blind eye to an affair either!'

'Why would I have an affair with Nabila? Have you asked yourself that?' Raj demanded, moving forward to scoop her gently up into his arms and return her with care to the lounger before stepping back to lean back lithely against the balcony wall.

'Because you still love her…' Zoe muttered ruefully.

'Why would I still love a woman who slept with another man behind my back?' Raj asked gently. 'Do you honestly believe I am so stupid that I would still blindly love a woman who was unworthy of my love and respect?'

Zoe reddened and her eyes evaded his. 'I'm not saying you're stupid, just that sometimes people can't control their feelings even when they *know* they should,' she framed uncomfortably.

'But that is not the case with Nabila. My love died the instant I realised how poorly I had judged her character. She was my first love,' Raj admitted grittily. 'At the age of twenty I also believed she would be my last love but I was very young and I was wrong. I couldn't continue to love a woman who lied and cheated once I saw her for what she was. I couldn't love a woman who only wanted me because I am wealthy and one day I will be King.'

'Well, if that's all true what were you doing holding hands with her?' Zoe demanded baldly, influenced against her will by the obvious sincerity of his self-defence.

'Before I left the palace yesterday, I received a phone call from a journalist and it was most illuminating…yes, I *know* you are impatient for an explanation but please bear with me to enable me to tell you the whole story,' Raj urged when she made a frustrated gesture with one tiny expressive hand. 'I learned from that call that Nabila had personally contacted him and given him the photos that proved the existence of our youthful romance.'

'*She* was behind the release of those photos to the gossip magazine?' Zoe exclaimed in surprise.

'Yes. I assume she wanted that information publicised as a first move in her desire to come back into my life. Evidently she assumed there would still be a place for her in my heart.' Raj's wide sensual mouth compressed. 'The journalist involved called to warn me yesterday that she was planning to wreck my marriage and had a photographer lined up in readiness.'

'Journalists love scandal. Why would he have warned you?' Zoe pressed suspiciously.

'Zoe…' Raj murmured softly. 'The gossip magazine was quite happy to publish old photos of a romance few people knew about but the owner, the journalist I mentioned, is a loyal Marabanian and he refused to get involved in framing me with Nabila in a seedy scheme likely to damage my marriage. That was a step too far for him and, instead of playing along, he warned me of her ambition to cause trouble.'

'Well, it doesn't look like the warning did you much good,' Zoe said drily.

'It put me on my guard and I took Omar with me on the trip. When I went to my hotel room that night, she was waiting for me in the bed and I had her removed. We didn't have a conversation either because I have nothing to say to Nabila,' Raj told her doggedly.

'Nothing?' Again, Zoe looked unimpressed by his claim but she was already thinking of the stunning brunette waiting in his bed for him. 'Was she undressed?'

Raj nodded.

'And you weren't even tempted?' Zoe prompted helplessly.

'No, but I think my protection team were,' he remarked wryly. 'Omar can confirm that nothing happened. He was also present at the table when she grabbed my hand.'

'Grabbed?' Zoe queried with a frown. 'But how

could Omar have been there when you were alone with her?'

'I wasn't alone with her. The photo is deceptive. Three of Nabila's colleagues were also at that table with us.' Raj dug out his phone and brought up the photo for her appraisal. 'And if you look…*there…* you can just about see the sleeve of the man sitting beside me.'

Her heart thumping hard at getting that close to him again, Zoe stared down at the photo and squinted until she too registered that there was indeed a tiny glimpse of what could only have been another arm at the very edge of the picture.

'Nabila arranged for her photographer to take that photo to suggest an intimacy that does not exist between us. When she grabbed my hand, I was so disconcerted I didn't react fast enough to evade the photographer. I was too *polite* to say what I wanted to say in front of other people,' he derided with sudden visible annoyance. 'I believed I had dealt with her in the hotel room the night before and that she would leave me alone, resenting the fact that I had rejected her invitation… I was wrong, for which I am heartily sorry. But I have *nothing else* to apologise for.'

'So you say…' Zoe muttered, fixedly studying his lean, darkly beautiful face while her brain sped over everything that he had explained, seeking a crack or a hole in his account of events. 'And how do you feel about her now?'

'What would I feel but heartfelt relief that she showed me what she was before I made the mistake of marrying her?' Raj countered wryly. 'Omar is downstairs waiting to act as my witness.'

Zoe swallowed hard on that assurance before an involuntary giggle was wrenched from her. 'Raj, if you killed someone, Omar would bury the body for you! You two are *that* close. Omar in the guise of a reliable witness is a joke!'

Raj dropped fluidly down on his knees beside the lounger and studied her with raw frustration. 'Then I will produce the other people at that table for your examination,' he swore with fierce determination.

Zoe adored him in that moment because she believed him, believed that he would go to any embarrassing length to prove his innocence. He had been warned about Nabila's plans and had assumed that he had taken sufficient precautions to protect himself but the devious brunette had still contrived to catch him out. He simply wasn't sly enough to deal with a woman that shameless, he was too honourable, too loyal, too honest, and that Nabila had attempted to use his very decency against him infuriated Zoe.

'No, that won't be necessary,' Zoe told him

tenderly. 'You don't need to embarrass yourself that way.'

'It wouldn't embarrass me if it gave *you* peace of mind,' Raj argued. 'That is all that matters here—'

'No, what really matters,' Zoe murmured with a new strength in her quiet voice, 'is that I *be-lieve* you.'

'But you said Omar is no good as a witness,' he reminded her in bewilderment.

'I was sort of joking,' Zoe muttered in rueful apology. 'I *do* believe that you have told me the truth.'

'Allah be praised,' Raj breathed in his own language.

'How long did it take you to get over Nabila?' Zoe asked then with helpless curiosity.

'Not very long once what I realised what an idiot I had been!' Raj confessed in a driven undertone. 'But the whole experience damaged me, and even before I met her I was already damaged by my mother's suicide. That made it difficult for me to trust *any* woman.'

Zoe ran soothing fingertips down from a high masculine cheekbone to the hard angle of his taut jaw. 'Of course, it did,' she whispered sympathetically. 'You were badly hurt when you were still a child and then hurt and humiliated by what happened with Nabila. I can understand that.'

'But you will probably *not* understand that I never had another relationship with a woman until I met you,' Raj admitted harshly. 'All I allowed myself was a succession of grubby one-night stands.'

'Grubby?' She questioned his wording.

'It *was* grubby when I compare those encounters to what I have found with you,' Raj confessed.

'And what have you found with me?' she whispered, her gaze held fast by the silvered darkness of his, heart pounding with anticipation, because in those eloquent eyes of his she saw what she had long dreamt of seeing but barely credited could be real.

'Love,' he said simply. 'Love like I never felt for anyone, certainly not for Nabila. That was a boy's love, this is a man's and you mean the whole world to me. I don't know how else to describe how very important you are to me...'

'You're doing great,' she mumbled encouragingly when he hesitated.

'I hate being away from you. I missed you when I went to bed last night and when I woke up this morning. Wherever you are feels like home. Whenever you smile, my heart lifts. At the beginning,' he breathed hoarsely, 'I believed it was only sexual attraction and I tried incredibly hard to resist you...but I couldn't. What I've learned since is that you are the very best thing that has ever happened to me and you make me amazingly happy.'

Zoe breathed in slow and deep and it was a challenge when her lungs were struggling for oxygen. He had just made all her dreams come true. He had just blown her every insecurity out of the water but she still had some questions. ‘So why, when I told you that I was pregnant, didn’t you tell me then how you felt?’

‘Because I didn’t know how you felt about me,’ Raj responded as though that were an obvious explanation. ‘And I had messed everything up with you from the start. I was worrying about you wanting to leave me and going back to the UK to get the divorce I had stupidly promised you, and wondering how I could possibly prevent that from happening. I have never been more relieved than when our unexpected but very much welcome baby gave us the excuse to stay together.’

‘I didn’t need an excuse,’ she told him then. ‘I didn’t want to leave you…well, probably since the honeymoon, maybe even sooner, I’m ashamed to admit. I fell in love with you weeks and weeks ago and knew it but I wasn’t going to tell you that *ever*.’

Raj sprang gracefully upright and lifted her up into his arms to sit back down on the lounger holding her tight, as if he feared she might make a sudden leap for freedom. ‘I denied my feelings for a long time and tried to hold back but you give me so much joy it is hard to hide it from you,’ he confided huskily. ‘That you return my love is almost more than I could ever have hoped for because I love you so much it burns in me like a fire…'

A knock sounded on the patio doors. Raj rose with her in his arms as the door opened.

'What the hell—?' Vivi began in shock when she saw them.

'Bad timing, Vivi,' Zoe interrupted sharply. 'My husband loves me and I'll see you at breakfast.'

Behind her Winnie laughed and tugged Vivi back. 'Yes, breakfast promises to be fun, Raj… with Grandad grouching and Vivi giving you suspicious looks, but if Zoe trusts you, you have my trust too.'

'You turncoat!' Vivi gasped but Winnie was inexorably dragging her out of the room.

'So, where were we?' Zoe prompted as Raj deposited her on the bed and went straight across the room to lock the bedroom door in a sensible move that delighted her. 'Ah, yes, you were saying that your love is like a fire.'

'More of an eternal flame,' Raj assured her poetically. 'You've got me for life.'

'Thank goodness for that. You see, I'm not a changeable woman,' she murmured softly, eyes gliding possessively over his lean, powerful length. 'I expect and demand for ever and ever, like in all the best fairy tales.'

'Perfect,' Raj murmured hoarsely, framing her flushed face with reverent hands as he stared down at her with unashamed adoration before claiming her pink pouting lips with passionate hunger.

And it was perfect for both of them as they left behind their doubts and fears and rejoiced in their newly discovered closeness and trust. Passion united them as much as love, every sense heightened for them both by the fear that they could have lost each other.

'I love you so much,' he breathed in a hoarse groan in the aftermath.

'I love you too,' she whispered, both arms wrapped possessively round him, a glorious sense of peaceful happiness powering her with a new surge of confidence.

EPILOGUE

EIGHTEEN MONTHS LATER Zoe laughed as she watched her year-old son lurch like a tiny drunk across the floor to greet his father, because he had only begun walking for the first time the day before. Raj had been really disappointed to miss those very first steps because he had been in Moscow on business and the video Zoe had sent had only partially consoled him. Now, he swept the toddler up into his arms with noisy sounds of admiration so that Karim's little face literally shone with his sense of achievement and his delight in his father's appreciation.

Raj was a great father, keen that his son would grow up with few of the royal restrictions and traditions that had held him back during his often lonely childhood. Karim was encouraged to play with other children and he was fortunate that his many cousins on both sides of the family were regular visitors. Even King Tahir unbent in Karim's energetic and sunny presence, but then the whole of Maraban was still reacting to Karim's birth as though he were an absolute miracle. That level of interest was a big weight for one little boy to carry on his shoulders and Zoe did everything she could to ensure that his upbringing was as normal and as un-starry as she could make it, even though they lived in a royal palace. Karim also had a pair of grandfathers, who sought to outdo each other with the very lavishness of their gifts.

Zoe was blissfully happy in her marriage. Raj made every day they were together worth celebrating. He loved her as she had never dreamt she would ever be loved and he gave her amazing support with everything she did. He had even made an effort to strengthen his relationships with her occasionally challenging family and was now her grandfather's favourite grandson-in-law, while Vivi had apologised for her initial doubts about Raj's suitability as a husband and fully accepted him, so that Zoe could relax and mix freely with her sisters and their husbands.

Zoe's fingers slid down to press gently against the very slight swelling beneath her sundress that signified that in a few months Karim would have company in the royal nursery. She had had an easy pregnancy and an easy birth with her son and was keen to have her children close together and complete their family while she was still in her twenties. Raj had wanted her to wait a little longer but she had persuaded him because Zoe adored babies and she hadn't wanted to wait when there was no good medical reason to do so.

'You look like a splash of sunlight when you wear yellow,' Raj murmured huskily as Karim was borne off by his nanny for his bath and he intercepted his wife before she could follow them. 'Our little Prince will manage without his parents for one bathtime.'

'But—' Zoe began.

'My son has to *share* you with me,' Raj pointed out, appraising her beautiful smiling face with all-male hunger. 'And this evening when your sisters arrive to celebrate your birthday with you, it'll be giggles and girl talk and I won't get a look-in.'

'Well, if you would just wait until bedtime that wouldn't be the case,' Zoe teased.

'I waited for bedtime the last time!' Raj groaned as he bent her back over one strong arm to engage in kissing a trail across her delicate collarbone that sent a highly responsive quiver through her slight body and flushed her cheeks. 'And you didn't come to bed until *three* in the morning!'

Zoe grinned. 'That'll teach you patience!'

'I'm no good at waiting for you,' Raj confessed, bundling her up into his arms with ease and heading for their bedroom. 'I'm not any better at not missing you when I'm away and I'm even worse at getting by without you in my bed.'

'You've only been away two days, but I missed you too,' Zoe confided with a helpless sigh of contentment as he brought her down on the bed. A little ripple of positively wanton anticipation gripped her as he began to remove his business suit, revealing that long bronzed, lithe and powerful physique she adored.

'I wonder if it's normal to have sex as often as we do,' she muttered abstractedly.

'It's a great healthy workout,' Raj assured her with unholy amusement. 'And wonderfully rewarding if done right.'

'No wonder I love you,' Zoe teased him back with dancing eyes. 'You always do it right!'

'But only with you.' Raj groaned with pleasure as she skimmed her hands over him, and kissed her with a raw, passionate love that made further discussion impossible.

* * * * *

If you enjoyed
The Sheikh Crowns His Virgin,
you're sure to enjoy the other two stories
in Lynne Graham's
Billionaires at the Altar trilogy!

The Greek Claims His Shock Son
The Italian Demands His Heirs

Available now!

And why not explore these other
Lynne Graham stories?

The Greek's Blackmailed Mistress
The Italian's Inherited Mistress

COMING NEXT MONTH FROM

Available June 18, 2019

#3729 THE GREEK'S PREGNANT CINDERELLA

Cinderella Seductions

by Michelle Smart

Tabitha is stunned to be gifted a ticket to Giannis's ball. But this untouched Cinderella ends up in his bed—utterly pleasured! She expects to return to her ordinary life...until Tabitha discovers a nine-month consequence!

#3730 HIS TWO ROYAL SECRETS

One Night With Consequences

by Caitlin Crews

For one passionate night in a stranger's arms Pia feels free...and then she learns she's carrying the Crown Prince of Atilia's twins! But Pia's true royal secret is that she's falling inescapably in love with her dark-hearted prince...

#3731 BOUGHT BRIDE FOR THE ARGENTINIAN

Conveniently Wed!

by Sharon Kendrick

Hired by Alejandro, executive Emily must redeem this playboy's reputation. She suggests he take a convenient wife to show he's changed. What she doesn't expect is Alejandro's insistence that *she* take on the role!

#3732 DEMANDING HIS HIDDEN HEIR

Secret Heirs of Billionaires

by Jackie Ashenden

Billionaire Enzo has never known a passion like the one he shared with Matilda. But she left abruptly... Now Matilda has reappeared—with his son! Enzo demands his heir, but will he claim vibrant Matilda, too?

HPCNM0619RA

#3733 HIS SHOCK MARRIAGE IN GREECE

Passion in Paradise

by Jane Porter

When tycoon Damen's convenient bride is switched at the altar for Kassiani, he's adamant their marriage will remain strictly business. He's too damaged for anything more... Yet will the intense passion of their honeymoon be his undoing?

#3734 AN INNOCENT TO TAME THE ITALIAN

The Scandalous Brunetti Brothers

by Tara Pammi

To uncover a business scandal, billionaire Massimo requires shy Natalie to play his fake fiancée. But this untamable Italian might have met his match in innocent Nat, who challenges him...and tempts him beyond reason!

#3735 WED FOR THE SPANIARD'S REDEMPTION

by Chantelle Shaw

The only way Rafael can become CEO is if he marries. He isn't the commitment kind, but he'll save single mother Juliet financially if she becomes his wife. But can Rafael keep their marriage purely for appearances?

#3736 RECLAIMED BY THE POWERFUL SHEIKH

The Winners' Circle

by Pippa Roscoe

Ten years ago, Mason was swept into an affair with Prince Danyl. Now he's back with a million-dollar demand she cannot refuse. Will their painful past be overcome by their intense desire?

Billionaire Enzo has never known passion like what he shared with Matilda. But she left abruptly... Now Matilda has reappeared—with his son! Enzo demands his heir, but will he claim vibrant Matilda, too?

Read on for a sneak preview of Jackie Ashenden's debut story for Harlequin Presents, Demanding His Hidden Heir.

"*Bueno notte*, Mrs. St George," Enzo said in that deep voice she knew so well, the one that had once been full of heat and yet now was so cold. "I think you and I need to have a little chat."

"A chat?" she said huskily, her chin firming, the shock and fear in her gaze quickly masked. "A chat about what?"

With an effort, Enzo dragged his gaze from her throat.

So, she was going to pretend she didn't know what he was talking about, was she? Well, unfortunately for her, he wasn't having it.

"I'm not here to play games with you, Summer," he said coldly. "Or should I say Matilda. I'm here to talk about my son."

Another burst of quicksilver emotion flashed in her eyes, but then it was gone, nothing but a cool wall of gray in its place. "Yes, that's my name. You don't have to say it like a pantomime villain. And as for a son… Well." Her chin came up. "I don't know what you're talking about."

"Is that how you're going to play this?" He didn't bother to temper the acid in his tone. "You're going to pretend you don't know anything about that child you just rescued downstairs? The child with eyes the same color as mine?" He took a step toward her. "Perhaps you're going to pretend that you don't know who I am either."

She held her ground, even though she didn't have anywhere to go, not when there was a wall behind her. "No, of course not." Her gaze didn't flicker. "I know who you are, Enzo Cardinali."

The sound of his name in her soft, husky voice made a bolt of lightning shoot straight down his spine, helplessly reminding him of other times when she'd said it.

HPEXP0619

0336

"Good." He kept his voice hard, trying not to let the heat creep into it. "Then if you know who I am you can explain to me why you didn't tell me that I have a son."

She was already pale; now she went the color of ash. But that defiant slant to her chin remained, the expression in her eyes guarded. "Like I said, I don't know what you're talking about."

Enzo's rage, already inflamed by his body's betrayal, curdled into something very close to incandescence, and it burned like fire in his blood, thick and hot.

He'd never been so angry in all his life, some distant part of him vaguely appalled at the intensity of his emotions—a reminder that he needed to lock it down, since his iron control was the only thing that set him apart from his power-hungry father.

But in this moment he didn't care.

This woman, this beautiful, sexy, infuriating woman, hadn't told him he had a son and, more, she'd kept it from him for four years.

Four. Years.

He took another step toward her, unable to help himself, the fire in his veins so hot it felt as if it was going to ignite him where he stood. "I see. So you are going to pretend you know nothing. How depressingly predictable of you."

"Simon is my son." Her hands had gone into fists at her sides and she didn't move, not an inch. "And H-Henry's." Her gaze was as cool as winter rain, but that slight stutter gave her away.

"No." Enzo kept his voice honed as a steel blade. "He is not. Those eyes are singular to the Cardinali line. Which makes him mine."

"But I—"

"How long have you known, Matilda? A year? Two?" He took another step, forcing her back against the wall.

Enzo put a hand on the wall at one side of her silky red head and leaned in close so she had no choice but to stare straight at him. "Look at me, *cara*. Look at me and tell me that you don't see your son staring back."